# IN THE BELLY OF THE EARTH

---

ROBERT L. FULLER

This is a work of fiction. Names, characters, organizations, places, events, and incidents are either products of the author's imagination or are used fictionally. Any resemblance to actual persons, living or dead, or actual events is purely coincidental.



Published by StoryDoor Books

ISBN-13: 978-0692942208 (StoryDoor Books)

ISBN-10: 0692942203

Cover design by Anthony Edwards Create.com

*For my wife*

"Whoever follows me will never walk in darkness but will have the light of life." John 8:12

# 1

Frederick Platt loved books more than anything. Simply adored them. Worshipped the very shelves they stood upon.

"I like the smell of the pages," he'd told his parents once when asked why he refused to part with a book at the dinner table. Pressing the binding to his nose he'd waxed eloquent like a chef describing a favorite dish. "Wood pulp pressed into paper then printed with ink..." he inhaled with relish "ahhhhh, nothing better."

His parents had glanced at each other with no small measure of concern, then returned to their pot roast and mashed potatoes as he resumed his reading.

Fred had always been a unique sort of boy. What three-year-old, for instance, memorizes the periodic table for fun? Or how many five-year-olds can spout off the Declaration of Independence with the ease of a nursery rhyme? The boy's mind was like a steel trap. His knowledge copious as a professor's.

Though more than a little sun-starved, things could be worse for the boy, his parents thought. At least he wasn't hyper or obese or, worst of all, addicted to a smart phone. Wasn't Einstein an outcast? And Edison a misfit? *Let the boy be*, they mused, as visions of Ivy League danced in their heads.

But even the most ardent parental resolve often crumbles in the face of social isolation.

"He has no friends," his mother said one night in bed, shoulder to shoulder with her husband, both of them staring at the ceiling. They wore matching pajamas and furrowed brows. "How could the boy not be lonely?"

"Calm yourself, Eunice," his father said, patting her leg. "I have an idea."

"What is it?"

"A few guys at the office have their sons in this outdoorsman troop called the Woodlanders. They have a camping trip this weekend open for new recruits."

"Allen, you can't be serious!"

"I'm nothing but."

"Freddy can hardly step outside without sneezing. And you know how he feels about formally-arranged social settings. He'll never go."

"What if I bribe him?"

"With what?"

"How about a new leather bound volume of Tolkien I found down at the used book store? It's illustrated and everything. Has a big foldable map of Middle Earth inside. He'll love it."

"Of course he will. But enough to strike out into the wilderness with a crowd of perfect strangers? I don't know."

"Just leave it to me, Eunice. It's about time the boy gets his nose out of his books and starts making friends. All this introversion can't be healthy."

The woman sighed, reached over and switched off the light. "I certainly hope you're right."

"WHAT?" Fred's fingers spasmed at the breakfast table just long enough to loose their hold on the book he was reading. It tipped forward and almost catapulted his entire bowl of cereal, milk and all, onto his lap. With eyes wide, he asked again. "You did what?"

Dad held his newspaper up with both hands, hiding his face. "I signed you up for the Woodlanders. You're going camping this weekend."

Mom refilled his orange juice and patted her son's trembling hand. "It'll be fun, Freddy. Just think of all the new friends you'll make."

The boy looked at her with pleading eyes, but quickly saw she was of one mind with his father. With frantic fingers, he began to scratch the skin of his forearms. "I think I'm getting hives," he said. "Stress can cause them, you know. Yeah...I must be really stressed out about this." He started shivering and then began coughing weakly into his hand, glancing up to see what effect such dramatics were having on his parents. Not much, apparently.

"It'll be good for you, son," his father said, lowering the paper. "It may not prove the most comfortable thing in the world. But why don't you at least give it a go and hold your judgments to the end?"

"But what about my books?"

"No books allowed," he said. "I want you interacting with actual flesh and blood humans."

"But...mom!" He turned to his mother, face crimson, veins popping out on his neck like worms writhing under his skin.

"The decision's been made, sweetheart," she said with a compassionate smile.

Fred could only sit there in utter shock.

THREE DAYS LATER, surrounded by trees and bugs and strangers, Fred pondered the injustice of the world. It wasn't so much the uniform (starchy pants and a button-down shirt that fit like he'd been stuffed into a burlap sack), or even the food (not bad for wilderness standards). It was the fabricated camaraderie; boys thrown together like a handful of roaches with hopes they might forge some lasting bonds. He'd never bonded with anyone. At least not anyone outside the page of some book.

Hunched on a tree stump on the edge of the campsite, he observed a cluster of boys as they pummeled a turtle with rocks. He'd read once about wolf pack behavior, and found the boys' interaction uncannily canine.

"Try to crack its shell," the tallest of the group said. His name was Craig. He had a head of hair the color and texture of a dirty mop and a merciless case of acne. Judging by his behavior, he was definitely the alpha male of the group. He stepped within five feet of the creature and threw a baseball-sized stone as hard as he could. The projectile struck the turtle with a sickening crack. Had not their troop leader showed up the next minute, the turtle would have been smashed to oblivion.

"Boys!" he shouted. "Stop this instant!"

Mr. Howard picked up the hapless creature and delivered it safely into the nearby woods. When he returned, his mouth and his mustache were frowning something terrible.

"We treat animals with respect," he said, shaking his

head and pointing to each boy in turn. "We live in harmony with nature. Understand?"

"Yes, Mr. Howard," every boy answered, though Fred could see Craig and his cronies mocking the man behind his back. When their leader walked off to gather wood for the evening's fire, Craig grew even more brazen.

"One with nature....one with the universe!" He raised his hands high and the other boys were in stitches, falling on the ground and clutching their sides. Fred thought it wasn't all that funny. He knew they were just trying to impress him. Increase their rank in the pack.

"I present to you," Craig announced, pulling a spray can from his backpack and holding it up for all to see, "my manly, anti-stink elixir. Puberty, gentlemen, is upon me."

The other boys mumbled with apparent envy and gathered close as Craig demonstrated the proper application of aerosol deodorant. Fred fought back a smile as half of them were enveloped in a bilious cloud.

"What are you grinning at, powder puff?" Craig shouted across camp. It took a moment for Fred to realize he was the object of the taunt.

"I'm sorry?"

"You will be sorry if you don't wipe that stupid look off your face. Haven't you ever seen a kid with testosterone? I bet you won't stink under your arms until tenth grade and won't shave until you're thirty."

Everyone laughed. Fred looked around hopefully for Mr. Howard, who was, of course, nowhere to be seen at the moment.

Craig stepped away from the others and walked right up to the stump where Fred still sat. He leaned down until his face was level with Fred's, his breath puffing out in sour gusts. "Mr. Leader's not here to help you, powder puff."

Before Fred could respond, he found himself shoved hard in the chest and flying backward. His shoulder hit a rock jutting up from the ground and his head smashed into a pinecone. His ears rang and his eyes watered.

"Oooohhhhh...." Craig jumped onto the stump and leaned over, sticking out his lip. "Is powder puff gonna cry? Does he need his wittle bwanket?"

Fred's head cleared just enough for him to notice how precarious the bully's position was at the moment. Without so much as a thought of the consequences, he swung his leg at Craig's ankles and knocked them clear into the air. Craig screamed, fell, and smashed his shoulder against the stump beneath him. Every pair of eyes stared wide as silver dollars as Craig, face flushed crimson, recovered himself and leapt upon Fred with lightning speed.

"Now you're gonna pay, powder puff!" he growled through clenched teeth, clutching Fred's uniform collar with a death grip.

"What in the world?" Mr. Howard dashed from the trees and descended upon them. Craig let go at once and fell upon the ground in instant tears. Everyone pointed to Fred with shouted accusations.

"He just kicked Craig for no reason!"

"Yeah! What gives?"

Of course, the only visible injury was Craig's—a long scrape along one ankle from Fred's hiking boots. Mr. Howard knelt at Craig's side as he babbled through a sheet of tears. Once their leader managed to clean up the wound with a wad of paper towels and a splash of water from his canteen, Craig finally stopped crying, though his chin still quivered. An act worthy of an Oscar, Fred thought.

"Tell me what happened," Mr. Howard said.

Craig pointed at Fred. "He kicked me."

"Is this true?" the man asked.

"Yes, but...."

"No buts...only answers."

Several boys chuckled and shook their rear ends from side to side.

Fred looked at the ground. "It's true, but..."

"See?" Craig crossed his arms over his chest and shook his head. "I say you send him home."

Mr. Howard scoffed. "I'm not going to ruin a trip we've had planned for six months just because you two can't get along. I'm sure this 'kick' was not unprovoked. Am I right?" He looked at Fred, and then at Craig, then nodded with a satisfied smirk.

"I thought so. Okay," he stood to his feet and grabbed both boys by the arm. "I'll tell you what I'm going to do." He led them to the far edge of camp, down a hill and to the center of the latrine, which was little more than a series of scattered mounds of dirt and a shovel.

"You're going to take turns leveling out the dirt and then you're going to lay down some lime, which I'll bring you in a little bit. I want this area smelling sweet as honeysuckle once you're done."

"I'm telling my Mom!" Craig said, kicking the ground. "This is cruel and unusual punishment."

"You go ahead and do that," Mr. Howard said. "I'd bet you a year's allowance she'd thank me like I was Moses." He let their arms drop and trudged back up the hill.

In the ensuing silence, the two boys stood side by side in a graveyard of excrement. The smell and the flies were thick in the stifling summer heat. Fred spotted the shovel leaning against a nearby tree. He took a deep breath, and carefully picked his way along like he was crossing a minefield. He'd read a whole book on germs the year before and knew all too well the nasty powers of bacteria. He sighed in relief once he reached the shovel, having successfully avoided contamination. Never in his life had he wanted a biohazard suit more than that moment.

"Did you know that bacteria can eat you alive?" he asked, more to keep his mind alert than engage in conversation.

Craig shook his head and moved to a patch of grass, where he sat down in a huff.

"It's true," Fred continued. "There's a kind of bacteria that eats up your flesh like a microscopic smorgasbord. And do you know how much bacteria lives in human feces?"

"Shut up," Craig mumbled.

"With the possibility of mutation....some bacteria can go airborne." Fred began the process of patting down the mounds with the underside of the shovel. "So if you think about it, we could be breathing in airborne, flesh-eating bacteria this very moment."

"I said shut up, powder puff."

Fred shrugged and continued with the work. For several minutes Craig simply stared at him, watching with narrowed eyes, like a snake - evil, coiled and ready to strike. Fred tried to tune out the death glare through a mental recitation of the elements.

*Actinium.*

*Aluminum.*

*Americium.*

*Antimony.*

*Argon.*

Fred had gotten all the way to Xenon by the time Mr. Howard returned with a five-pound bag of lime. He noticed Craig sitting on the ground and his frown deepened.

"Get up!" He tossed the bag into the boy's arms, almost

knocking him backward. A cloud of white powder emanated from the bag, hovering about his head.

"My asthma!" Craig cried out.

Mr. Howard was unmoved. "You don't have asthma."

"I think I do," Craig began to wheeze. He dropped the bag and gripped his neck with both hands. His eyes bulged out like a squeeze toy.

The troop leader stole a glance at Fred and gave him a secretive little grin that made Fred feel a lot better. Craig wasn't fooling Mr. Howard after all. When Craig was through with his faked respiratory emergency and it was clear no one was calling an ambulance, he frowned and lowered his hands.

"How long till' we're finished?" he asked.

"Well," Mr. Howard said. "Considering the fact that you've yet to lift a finger while Fred here has done all the work, I'd say you won't be done until the entire area is dusted white. Use the whole bag...distributed evenly. Don't come back until it's done or I'll make you start over from scratch. Understand?"

Craig's face reddened, but he did as was told. By dusk the latrine was flat as a giant checkerboard and white as a January morning. As the boys made their way back to camp in growing darkness Craig finally spoke.

"I'm gonna end you, you know."

Instant chills ran up Fred's spine and lifted the hairs on the back of his neck. It wasn't so much the words, either. It was how he said it. So calm. So cool. As if he was talking about eating a cheeseburger.

With hands shoved in his pockets, head tilted back in thought, Craig continued. "I'd have to get you somewhere completely isolated...where no one could see us. That's where I'd do it. And you'd be lost forever. Your picture slapped on the side of a milk carton years before they found your bones."

*Surely he's kidding.* Fred thought. *He's just trying to freak me out.* But for a moment there, Fred felt sure he was walking beside the devil himself.

A hundred yards short of camp, Craig stopped and grabbed the edge of Fred's shirt. With eyes wide, Fred turned to look, thinking he would see a monster, smell his dragon breath, look into a pair of glowing red eyes.

But Craig was smiling, and his grin widened as he took in Fred's face, read it out as clearly as a newspaper's headlines.

"Oh my gosh! You actually believed I was serious. Priceless!" He busted out laughing at the top of his lungs and slapped Fred so hard on his shoulder it shook him all the way down to his shoes. "Come on, dude," he said with a seemingly light-hearted shrug and led the way back. Fred stood motionless as the other boy's footsteps crunched away over gravel and dirt, fading into the sound of cricket song.

Staring after Craig, Fred couldn't help but wonder:

*Was he really joking?*

*Was he really?*

# 2

The next morning, all twelve boys of Troop 354 clustered at the base of a fifty-foot cliff for their maiden foray into rock climbing. Mr. Howard had spent hours setting up ropes and clips and carabineers to ensure the boys' safety. He now stood before them in his harness and helmet, ready to show them proper form.

"Remember, boys, this is serious business. Any of you start messing around and you could fall to your deaths."

Fred's heart rate sped up, and he wondered if such stark diction was Woodlander policy, to scare feckless boys into compliance.

"Your harness thingy looks like underwear!" Craig blurted, followed by a burst of laughter quickly silenced by the cold glare of their leader.

"Another word from you and I'll have you digging dung all afternoon."

Craig snickered, but nodded his head.

"Okay then..." For the next several minutes, Mr. Howard explained a step-by-step strategy of climbing a straight-faced cliff side. He completed his instruction with a dexterous demonstration, reaching the top of the cliff in less than two minutes. All of the boys gawked upward, squinting into morning sunlight.

"Who wants to go first?" he yelled down from the heights.

No one volunteered.

"Come on! Get some backbone, will ya? Someone speak up before I have to start picking."

To everyone's collective relief, Craig finally raised his hand. "I'll go."

For a millisecond Mr. Howard frowned in irritation at his first volunteer, but nodded all the same. "Okay then. Let's get you roped up." He rappelled back down to the troop.

Once Craig was ready, Mr. Howard had hardly given the go ahead before the boy sprang onto the rock and sped up its face as quick and easy as a spider. He reached the top almost as fast as the grown man had. Everyone cheered and clapped and whistled. Craig waved like the king of the world, and then rappelled down in five sweeping leaps. When his feet hit the ground, he grinned in victorious pride and undid his harness.

"No big deal," he boasted.

Emboldened, the rest of the boys clawed their way to the front of a line leading to Mr. Howard. He smiled at their sudden courage and attended to each one by one. No boy climbed as swift and smooth as Craig had, but all had immense amounts of fun traversing a vertical wall for the first time in their adolescent lives.

All, that is, except for Fred.

He hadn't rushed to the front of the line when it formed, but had lingered on the fringes, hoping to avoid a turn. Yet as the line shrunk there seemed no way of escape. A stinging case of heartburn invaded his esophagus as cold sweat beaded his forehead.

Finally he found himself alone, staring up at Mr. Howard.

"Ready?" the man said, his eyebrows raised in expectation.

"I'm not sure."

"What do you mean?"

"I mean I'm not sure how safe this is. I've read some pretty nasty statistics about rock climbing injuries."

A smattering of laughter filled the air behind him. He felt all eyes upon his back.

"Fred," Mr. Howard smiled with a touch of exasperated condescension. "Do you actually think I would put you in deliberate danger?"

"Not deliberate. Of course not. But you did mention the possibility of plummeting to our deaths."

He rolled his eyes. "Just a bit of exaggeration to keep you guys sober, that's all. I promise, you'll love it."

"Come on, Fred, go for it!" someone shouted.

"It's totally awesome," another encouraged.

"Is powder puff gonna chicken out?"

Mr. Howard looked over Fred's head and pointed. "Not another word, Craig, understand?"

But the boys were laughing now. More and more by the moment.

"I can't do it," Fred said, staring steady into Mr. Howard's eyes.

"You have to."

"I can't."

"Why?"

"I'm afraid of heights. Of falling. Of hitting the ground

and snapping my spine in two. Of living my life in a wheel chair and sucking food from a straw."

"Chicken!" Craig shouted. Mr. Howard looked up again, acid in his expression. By now the rest of the boys were chiming in.

"If he doesn't want to go, then give someone else another turn!"

"Come on, Mr. Howard!"

"Powder Puff needs his bwanket."

Their leader finally looked at his watch, shrugged, and consented not to force Fred into something he didn't want to do.

"You would have loved it," he said as he packed up their things.

"I doubt that very much," Fred answered.

LUNCH CONSISTED of wonder bread bologna sandwiches, potato chips, and one fruit roll-up each, washed down with lukewarm Capri-Suns. Once they'd eaten and rested in their tents for a bit, Mr. Howard commanded all to don their swimsuits for a dip in the swimming hole.

The Buffalo River ran cold and cloudy-green alongside the campground, overlooked by a four hundred foot wall of limestone. The troop ran screaming and laughing down the grassy hillside leading to the water, diving headfirst into the currents. Mr. Howard barked a series of typical warnings, but allowed the general chaos as the boys splashed and thrashed about. He set out a lawn chair on the pebbled shore and popped open a Mountain Dew before settling in as lifeguard. Several minutes passed before he noticed Fred sitting in the shade of an oak tree a rock's throw upstream.

"What are you doing?" he shouted over the din.

Fred shrugged his cream white shoulders, and cradled a beach towel to his chest. "I'm not into swimming."

"Are you joking?" Mr. Howard asked, baffled even to hear such a thing. He knew that if the boy didn't swim soon, the hounds would descend and rip him to shreds no matter how hard he tried to stop them. Still, maybe a little peer pressure would do the kid some good? If it got him in the water, what was the hurt of some friendly ridicule?

Not surprisingly, it was Craig who took notice of Fred's absence first.

"What's the matter, powder puff? Can't swim?" He waded upstream until he stood ten feet from Fred. Others followed, ready to pounce as well.

Fred looked at Mr. Howard for help, but the Scout leader just stared at something on the far side of the river as if he hadn't noticed. He sipped his beverage. Craig seized the moment at once.

"Look at him, guys," he said. "He's white and squishy as a marshmallow. And he doesn't know how to swim."

"Yeah!" others chimed in lamely. "He's like...white and stuff....like a marshmallow."

"Should we throw him in the water?" Craig asked.

"Yeah!"

"Let's do it!"

Fred glanced at his erstwhile adult savior, but Mr. Howard still sat there, seemingly aloof.

Craig walked dripping out of the water until he loomed over Fred. Fred didn't look up or say a word.

"You're a scared little powder puff marshmallow who doesn't know how to swim," Craig said.

Other boys gathered behind him, sneering.

"Grab him!" Craig commanded. "Throw him in the water!"

Fred barely escaped their attempt, fleeing to where Mr. Howard sat.

"Aren't you going to do something?" Fred asked the man.

Mr. Howard looked up. "They just want you to swim," he said blandly. "If you got in on your own, this would die down instantly. Right, Craig?"

Craig was so shocked to find himself suddenly in league with Mr. Howard that his jaw actually dropped. Recovering himself, he straightened up tall, as if instantly ten years older, and looked down his nose at Fred.

"That's right," he said. "All of this would go away if powder puff here would swim."

But Fred was not about to be swayed, no matter who was against him. He set his feet firm, clenched his jaw, and told all within earshot his intentions. "I will personally bite anyone who touches me. That is a promise."

"Ooooohhhh!" Craig said, waving his hands in mock warning. "We've got a live one here, folks. He's dangerous. The marshmallow has teeth. Be careful."

"I promise anyone who touches me...." Fred's eyes were wide and flashing. "You will regret it."

Right as the mob began to move forward, Mr. Howard finally intervened, rising from his chair to stand between Fred and his persecutors. "That's enough! It's clear he doesn't want to swim. Everyone back in the water."

They mumbled in disappointment, but obeyed, returning to their splashing and underwater games. All, save for Craig, who stood there, grinning.

"Saved by the skin of your teeth, powder puff. Lucky you."

"Get back in, Craig. Now." Mr. Howard pointed to the water.

With a dark chuckle the brute slowly turned around and did what he was told.

Fred moved back to his spot under the tree and sat down, trying hard to keep it together. Tears threatened to break free, but he fought them tooth and nail. He'd already been labeled a coward. The last thing he needed now was to look like a blubbering fool.

For the rest of the afternoon, the river remained a playground. Fred studied the other boys as they rollicked about, dunking one another beneath the currents, playing hide and seek amidst overhanging vines on the opposite shore. It was beyond him why Mr. Howard did nothing to thwart such foolish behavior. Didn't they realize the concentration of spiders in such an area, not to mention snakes? What if one of them was bitten by a water moccasin? Or a black widow? Such carelessness was negligent at best, and downright idiotic at worst. Someone could die. Someone like Craig.

Fred let his thoughts drift into a daydream. What would that bully look like poisoned? Shivering and pale and feverish with wide-eyed agony, no doubt. Fred felt a rush of curiosity, then a wave of guilt, forcing the fantasy from his mind.

At half past five, Mr. Howard stood from his lawn chair and blew a whistle hanging from a shoelace around his neck.

"Alright boys," he said. "Time to get out and head back to camp. We're having sloppy joes tonight and I gotta get to cooking that meat. Hurry up now!"

At the mention of dinner, the troop erupted into hungry cheers and bounded from the water. Within seconds, the river was emptied of everything but fish and crawdads. Fred stood up and, not wanting to trail behind the mob, took a shortcut back to camp through a stand of cedar trees. He had just reached the edge of the clearing when he walked straight into an enormous spider web strung across the trail. So gargantuan was the web that it enveloped his entire head like a net. He stumbled forward, almost face-planting in the dirt, and pulled at the sticky fibers clinging to his face and hair. He felt something on his ear, and then his cheek, a flurry of spindly legs with a fat body hanging between them. With a bellow and a scream, he dashed forward, spinning about like a top and clawing at the creature on his face. Right into the center of camp he fled, crying and screaming and spinning. At some point the spider had fallen free, but Fred kept on flailing. Every last boy of the troop gathered round as if watching a sideshow. When Fred tripped and fell to the ground they clustered even closer to see what had happened.

"Look everyone," Craig said in his most insidious voice yet. "Powder puff is scared of his own shadow."

Raucous laughter.

Fred lay there, gazing up at a dozen mocking faces. He imagined a horde of demons would have been milder by comparison. He clambered to his feet, face smeared with tear-moistened mud. They laughed all the harder at the pitiful sight of him.

"Shut up!" he yelled as his face grew scarlet under the coating of mud. "Just shut up!"

Fred shoved his way out of the circle and took off running. Laughter lingered in the summer air behind him. He fled, wishing with all his might that he could be somewhere, anywhere else than on this trip with these boys in these woods.

# 3

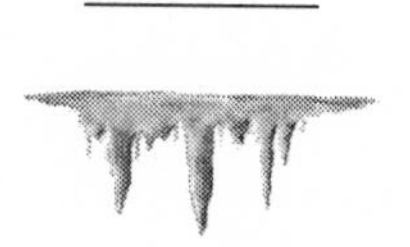

Leaves and branches slapped against his face as he ran. His tears were too thick now for him to see much of anything. It was just a trail leading up and away from the river, anyway. But onward he went, even as the sun caressed the western lip of the river's canyon.

Why had he even come on the stupid camping trip? He hated the Woodlanders, loathed the outdoors, and found the company of the first and being in the second as enjoyable as a case of poison ivy. His parents had coaxed him into joining and the only reason he'd said yes was to stifle their nagging once and for all.

Suddenly the trail dead-ended at the foot of the cliff they'd climbed that morning. Fred stopped, leaned over with his hands on his knees and gasped for air. If only he could have run all the way home. At least there he wouldn't have to listen to Craig's mocking, or hear the derisive laughter of his campmates.

Fred looked up in the waning light and studied the cliff. There were no ropes now. No hooks and harnesses to keep one tethered to stone, yet he felt a sudden and surprising urge to climb. With no one to watch him, there was no risk of being made fun of. No one could call him powder puff, or marshmallow, or any kind of nasty thing. He gritted his teeth and stepped to the base of the bluff, taking hold of the lowest knob of rock. He pulled himself upward, gained a foothold, and began to climb. He would prove that he could do it, that he could take the cliff without ropes all the way to the top. Even Craig wouldn't risk such a thing. No one would.

Thirty seconds and eight feet later he glanced downward and froze. Shutting his eyes tight, he hugged the rock face as if he were a hundred feet up. His hands began to sweat, his muscles to tremble. And then, like some wicked thing had yanked him backwards, he fell. The crash upon ground knocked the breath from his lungs.

For five straight minutes, he lay there whimpering. Through a canopy of a thousand leaves the sky faded from orange to red. It would be dark soon, and his flashlight was back in the tent. He had no choice but to pull himself together, stand to his feet, and return to camp to face whatever ridicule awaited him there.

*I can't do this,* he thought, blinking tears from his eyes. Finally, he stood to his feet, brushed the dirt from his clothes and turned back toward camp. Minutes later, as he drew near to the tents and the fire, he heard the laughter of the boys, cut into by the occasional barking of Mr. Howard. He slowed his pace and waited in the shadows beyond the lantern light. The smell of cooking meat lingered in the air, instantly reminding him of his hunger. He licked his lips and stepped forward just in time to hear their leader declare his displeasure.

"If that boy doesn't come back in five minutes and I have to go searching for him while my dinner gets cold...I will be less than pleased. Has Powder....err, Fred come back yet?"

After a scattered muttering of no's, Fred retreated back into the darkness, stunned at such calloused neglect. Why didn't the man stop cooking long enough to search for him? What if he'd broken his neck falling from that cliff? They'd have found his corpse the next morning, cold beneath a slick sheen of dew.

Fred sighed and ambled up a trail to the north of camp, rounding the edge of the latrine. When he heard someone approaching, he slipped behind a tree to hide.

It was almost dark now, but he could tell it was Craig. There was no mistaking his oversized frame or head of tight, curly hair. The bully was mumbling something to himself, obviously upset, even frantic. Fred could just make out some of his words as the other boy grabbed the shovel and began to dig a hole in the loosened dirt.

"Please no....please no," Craig begged the air. Once a hole was dug, the boy crouched low, struggling with something in the dark that Fred could not see. Then Craig started hissing a string of curse words and Fred's mouth fell agape. He'd never heard such language outside of television before. Still mumbling and cursing to himself, Craig stood back up, wadded something up into a ball and dropped it in the hole. When he grabbed the shovel again to toss great heaps of soil into the hole he'd dug, Fred could see him glancing in the direction of camp. What was he doing? Why was he so nervous? Once finished, Craig patted down the dirt with the back of the shovel, wiped his hands on his shirt, and ambled away as if nothing had happened.

Fred waited until he was gone, then moved to the newly-filled hole. He wasn't positive what he would find. But he could guess. Before he had much time to think, he took the shovel and dug up what Craig had tried to hide. There in the last remnants of dusky light, he saw a flash of white, and grimaced as a sudden waft of odor met his nostrils. The smell was immediate and awful, but Fred found himself smiling.

The mighty Craig had messed his pants.

An idea formed inside his head. It would be an act of cruelty, to be sure, but one that might serve to repay all the ridicule he'd suffered on the trip. For a split second, he sensed a small voice in his head urging him to stop what he was doing that instant, but his resistance soon fell sway to his greater thirst for revenge.

What would have happened if he'd just dropped the underwear right then and there and returned to camp? After undergoing some more ribbing and teasing for running away, would he have gone home the next day, sprinted into the arms of his parents, and gone on with normal life? Impossible to know. In the end, Fred made his irrevocable choice and marched straight back to camp with Craig's soiled underwear waving like a flag in the breeze from the shovel's metal point.

"Everyone look!" he shouted as he walked into the full light of a blazing campfire. A dozen boys turned their heads, including Craig.

"Guess who messed their pants and tried to hide the evidence?" Fred shouted.

Instantly, the troop boys jumped to their feet and surrounded him, chuckling and pointing and holding their noses.

"Who did the deed?" someone asked.

"We'll call him Brownie boy!" someone else said.

Everyone exploded in laughter. Fred grinned. He'd never gotten such attention from other kids, at least without being victimized himself. Now he held the reins. It felt shockingly good. Beaming with delight, his eyes drifted toward the fire and the only one left behind sitting in its light.

Craig.

He was not laughing with the others, was only staring straight at Fred with wide, pleading eyes. Craig shook his head and mouthed the word *please.*

But it was far too late for that. Far too late for begging and pleading. That door had shut forever. The others were already grabbing the handle of the shovel, wrenching it from Fred's fingers. The underwear fell to the ground. Boys leapt out of the way.

"Don't touch it!" they cried.

"You'll get contaminated!"

A brave soul, short with freckles and curly red hair, crept close enough to pull up the elastic waistband, revealing the name written in faded permanent ink upon the tag. His mouth fell open. He looked up at the others, then over at Craig, whose head was already buried in his hands.

"Well?" someone asked.

"Whose is it?"

Fred clamped his mouth shut to stifle a chuckle. Lacking an easy escape, his mocking laugh swelled up his chest. It was just too good. Too perfect. How the mighty do fall! Finally, as if he were the accuser in a courtroom, he raised his arm and pointed at Craig.

It was as if the very air had been sucked free of oxygen. Several boys actually gasped aloud. Others covered their mouths as they gawked at their former leader hugging himself as the fire's flames flickered in front of him. When they saw that Craig offered no defense, but only stared at the ground in shame, the other boys knew his guilt was sure. And then, like a dam bursting, screams of laughter poured forth and swept away Craig's reputation like so much debris before a flood. One moment he had been all but worshipped by the other boys. And the next, derided like a leper.

Fame is a fickle friend.

They encircled him and began to chant.

"Brownie boy! Brownie boy!" they said faster and faster and louder and louder. Someone took the shovel and scooped up the underwear to wave it about in rhythm. It took well over a minute for Mr. Howard to take notice from the camp kitchen. He left his pan of frying meat on the propane stove and marched to the fireside, bristling.

"Boys!" he shouted. "What in the world is going on? Put that down this instant!"

Someone flung the underwear right at Craig. It careened off his forehead and landed in the coals of the fire, immediately smoking and then bursting into flames.

"Poop smoke! Run for your lives!" someone yelled, sending the troop screaming and laughing in all directions. His eyes wide as he tried to make sense of it all, Mr. Howard stood there at Craig's side as the boy began to sob.

"What's the matter, Craig?" Mr. Howard asked.

But Craig could not answer, could not even speak. He hid his face in his meaty hands and cried like a baby.

Fred saw it all from a stone's throw away. He hadn't joined the others in their ridiculous chant. He hadn't moved a muscle since he'd looked into Craig's eyes. And seeing him now break down in the awkward arms of Mr. Howard was about the most pitiful thing he had ever seen. It was all his fault, this sweet revenge, and it went bitter all the way down.

# 4

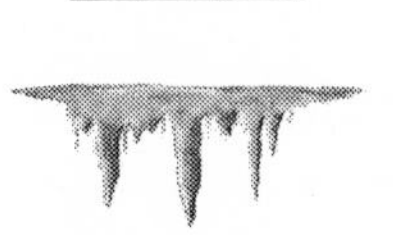

Fred couldn't sleep.

It wasn't the rock-hard ground beneath him, or the mosquito trapped in his tent, feasting on his hemoglobin. It wasn't even the two other boys on his right and left who snored in tandem like a rumbling tennis match.

It was Craig.

The memory of his pleading had haunted Fred long into the night. How Craig had seemed to shrink as the boys danced around him, chanting "Brownie Boy," a name he would doubtless find hard to escape for years to come.

He pulled the sleeping bag over his head and switched on his flashlight. The bright yellow glow against the nylon calmed his nerves. Darkness left far too much to the imagination.

How he wished it was already morning and they were packing up to leave. He'd get home and tell his parents how awful it had been. He'd beg them to let him out of the Woodlanders once and for all.

When Fred finally drifted off to sleep, it seemed only

seconds later when his eyes flew open. Bluish predawn light seeped through the roof of the tent.

"Fred?" someone whispered from outside.

"What?" he whispered back.

"Come out here...I want to talk to you." It was Craig. Fred swallowed, but did not answer.

"I'm not mad," the other said. "I promise. I deserved what happened. I can see that now. So come out here. I want to show you something."

The voice he was hearing right now sounded honest, almost regretful. This was not the voice of one who made a career out of ridicule. It held no brutal edge. Maybe Craig was really telling the truth. Maybe the act of the night before, though cruel and unusual, had actually served to cure a bully of his tyranny, show him the error of his ways. Fred had certainly read enough books where that kind of thing had happened to believe it.

"Just a sec," Fred said and pulled on his clothes. He quietly unzipped the tent so as not to wake the others and stepped out into cool morning air. Craig was standing there with a walking stick and a smile.

"Want to go see something cool?" he asked, his voice barely above a murmur.

"The sun hasn't even risen yet," Fred whispered.

"I know...but if we don't go now we won't be back before breakfast."

Fred took a deep breath, held it in his lungs. It'd be a nice way to bury the hatchet, he thought. Start over with Craig.

"Okay," he said, exhaling through his nose. "I'll go."

"Awesome!" Craig slapped him on the back. "Now get your shoes on and let's get out of here. I don't want Mr. Howard waking up to stop us. Don't forget your flashlight."

Twenty minutes later, they were half a mile upriver, moving along the shore until the trail turned sharply to the left, parallel to a boulder-strewn creek bed. Craig walked a few feet ahead of Fred, talking up a storm as dawn brightened the eastern sky.

"My Dad told me these mountains are honeycombed with caves. Most of them undiscovered. He said even a tiny little hole in the ground can open up into something huge if you know where to look."

Fred didn't like where this was going. "Don't you think we should get back?" he asked. "Breakfast is probably ready by now."

"We're almost there."

Five minutes later, they stood at the base of a deep ravine. Craig pointed several hundred feet up an incline where a cluster of car-sized boulders clung to the side of the mountain. "The surprise is up there. It won't take long to see."

"Are you sure about this?" Fred asked.

"Absolutely. This is going to be the coolest thing you've ever seen."

Suddenly doubting Craig's apparent enthusiasm, Fred searched the other boy's face for any hint of sarcasm or remnant of cruelty. But he saw none of either. The guy truly seemed as cordial and genuine as a tried and true gentleman.

He forced a smile. "Lead on, then."

Craig nodded with satisfaction. "All right! But just know it's gonna get dirty!" He stepped off the trail and started up the incline, picking his way between underbrush and scattered rocks. Fred did his best to follow, but the going was rough. He almost twisted his ankle twice and barely avoided tumbling backward. When they reached the boulders, Fred was completely out of breath. He plopped down on his rump to suck in some badly-needed oxygen.

Craig moved to the far side of one of the gargantuan rocks and gave a victory shout. "Found it!" he said. "There's hardly a soul alive who knows about this sink hole...and here we are!"

In no way, shape, or form did Fred like the sound of the word "sinkhole", but he said nothing to squelch his companion's delight.

"So what are we gonna do?" he asked.

"What do you think we're gonna do? I didn't bring you up here just to look at a stupid hole. We've already done that plenty of times in the latrine."

"True...but is it safe?"

"Of course it's safe! Chill out."

Fred wasn't sure if the other's definition of safety held much credence in the situation. But he saw no way out without giving offense. And he actually found himself wanting Craig to like him, to think he was brave. He stood and joined the other boy beside the opening in the ground.

If he hadn't known what it was, he wouldn't have thought much of it, even if he'd passed it on the trail. Not an inch wider than two feet across and hidden under a lip of rock. Easily missed if you didn't know where to look. Craig lowered to his belly and squirmed his way inside, as if the earth had swallowed him whole.

Fred couldn't believe what he was doing as he lay on his belly as well and followed the other below ground. The passage was just large enough to squeeze through, half full of dirt and rotting leaves. In an instant Fred's claustrophobia and germaphobia conspired together to spike his heart rate to almost double. He switched on his flashlight as he wriggled down, trying not to inhale microbial bacteria in the dust and soil.

"I don't think I can do this," he shouted down the passage. All he could see was the bottom of Craig's shoes several feet ahead.

"Just a little ways more..." Craig called back. His voice was muffled, as if spoken through a folded towel. "The tunnel gets bigger the further you go. I'll be able to stand up here pretty soon."

Fred moved on in a military crawl until the ceiling angled sharply upward, where Craig stood waiting with a dirt-smudged grin. He offered his hand and pulled Fred to his feet.

"This is where it starts to get good."

Before Fred could offer protest, the other boy darted down the passage. It was as large as a corridor, descending at almost thirty degrees. Fred watched the beam of Craig's flashlight bounce away into nothingness. He took a deep breath and followed.

Visions of Jules Verne's Journey to the Center of the Earth slithered about in Fred's mind as they moved deeper into the earth. It was still getting cooler. He heard Craig shouting up ahead, though he failed to catch the words due to the cacophony of echoes. Then, to his relief, he found the other boy had stopped. At first, Fred thought a wall of rock blocked the way, but when Craig stepped aside he saw the real reason they could not move on.

An abyss.

"Shine your light into the dark. Let's see if we can see anything down there."

Both boys raised their flashlights side by side, but the twin beams were devoured by the inky blackness below them.

"Wow," Craig said. He reached in his pocket, pulled out a quarter and flicked it into the dark. They waited several seconds before a distant *clink, clink, clink* marked the coin's landing.

"That room down there must be huge!" Craig said, shaking his head in wonder.

"Pretty amazing." Fred nodded, paused for as long as he could stand, then said, "So...ready to get back?"

Craig shook his head. "One more thing to see. It's on the floor of the cave. You need to stand on the ledge and look down with your flashlight."

"Are you serious?"

"Totally....you won't regret it."

"And then we can leave?"

"Sure. That's right."

Fred did as he was told, stepped forward with one hand touching the wall and looked out and over the drop-off. He pointed his flashlight straight down.

"I can't see much," he said. "What am I looking for?"

Two hands shoved him from behind and sent him flailing over the ledge, down and down into darkness.

# 5

Fred could not tell if his eyes were open or closed. He lay flat on cold, wet stone and stared up into perfect blackness. What had happened? He remembered lying warm and safe in his sleeping bag that morning. But now he was here, blind, his skull pounding as if he'd been struck with a hammer on the back of his head. He rubbed his eyes and blinked over and over, trying to recall what had happened. Still nothing but blackness, of both memory and sight...

*Craig!*

They had been on a hike. Craig had shown him the tunnel. They had crawled inside. And then...

It all became clear in a rush of understanding, and then, panic. Fred rolled over onto his stomach and pushed himself to all fours.

"Craig!" he tried to shout, but his voice seemed little more than a croak. He sucked in a lungful of air and yelled as loud as he could. "Craig!"

But there was no response. His voice was swallowed up

in the darkness. He squeezed his eyes shut and tried to slow his breathing. It had been an accident. Had to be.

"Craig....I'm okay. I'm not hurt. Everything's okay!"

He waited for an answer. But the only sound in the dark was his own breathing. Panic rose like bile in his throat. He tried to calm himself with thoughts of Craig running to get help. Surely, it wouldn't be long before Craig returned with Mr. Howard. Everything would be fine then. Everything would be fine.

Where was his flashlight? Fighting panic, he crawled around on all fours, sweeping his hands about in search of the metal cylinder. When he realized how easily he could fall into another unseen hole he froze and gripped the stone floor with his fingers. Fred rolled carefully onto his back as if he were perched on the edge of a canyon cliff, and focused on his breathing - slowly in through the nose, slowly out through the mouth, repeat. Again and again.

He started counting seconds and minutes. If Craig had run off to get help, he should be back within half an hour. But hadn't he been knocked unconscious? How long had he been out? The rescue party could be crawling down the tunnel that very moment.

Fred held his breath and listened. Water dripped somewhere in the blackness - a lonely, icy sound. But there was no hint of anyone crawling through a tunnel. Blackness pressed close about him - a veil of impenetrable tar.

When he reached fifteen minutes of counting, his teeth began to chatter. It was the first time he'd realized how cold he was. Shock had numbed him, but his senses were slowly returning. At thirty minutes, his entire body was shivering.

Where were they?

At an hour and a half, he gave up counting and resumed

his search for the flashlight, this time staying on his stomach like he was doing a military crawl. He stretched his arms out for any signs of changing terrain. His flashlight couldn't be far.

As he moved around in widening circles, the flat wet stone under his questing fingers grew riddled with chunks of rock and small boulders. Here and there the path was blocked by a stalagmite rising from the ground, a cave formation birthed from a trillion drops of mineral-laced water falling from the ceiling above. These formations grew more concentrated the further he went along, like teeth barricading further searching. Soon, it seemed, everywhere he moved the path was clustered with the unfamiliar shapes. He tried not to panic, but hot tears came quickly. Fear mingled with dread infused with misery washed over him and left him sobbing as he inched along the rugged ground.

Turning swiftly to the left, he smashed his head against a shaft of rock. He cried out and lurched backward by instinct, inadvertently slipping off a shallow ledge and into a pool of knee-deep water. Stabs of frigid pain assaulted his skin. He cried out in shock, his body one big spasm seeking escape from the life-sucking cave water.

His chattering and shivering grew more violent than ever as he pulled himself out of the pool and onto flat stone. He collapsed, too weary to move another muscle.

It was then, with warm snot still dripping down his face, that he somehow drifted off to sleep.

When he awoke, everything was so quiet. So still. He forgot for one blissful moment where he was. But the darkness reminded him soon enough.

How much time had passed? He could have been lying

there for hours. What if the rescue party had come while he slept? What if they'd called out to him and he hadn't heard? A myriad of terrifying "what if's" swirled in his head like a tempest. But then, the worst idea of all crept in and planted its claws in the remnant of his sanity.

What if a rescue wasn't coming at all? What if Craig had pushed him on purpose and left him there to die? Craig was the only one who knew where he was. He could have marched right back to camp and acted ignorant as a newborn child as to Fred's absence.

Fred thought back to how suddenly Craig had turned nice. One moment he had suffered utter humiliation at Fred's hands and the next he had been all buddy-buddy. Suddenly, he was sure that had all been an act. A cold-blooded ploy to get him alone so Craig could exact his revenge.

*Stupid!* Fred ridiculed himself. *You stupid ignoramus!*

Hadn't Craig told him about his intentions to kill him? He'd practically laid out his plan after they'd cleaned the latrine. He'd laughed it off as a joke, then. But it wasn't a joke. Not at all. Fred was more sure than ever that Craig not only had had the intention to do away with him, but every ounce of necessary gall and cruelty to see it through.

With a cry of rage and terror at his realization, he leapt to his feet, and began to run. If only he could reach the edge of the cave, touch the wall, somehow try and climb his way out.

His foot caught a lip of stone and he fell face first onto the ground, very nearly breaking his nose. He rolled over in defeat and let his arms fall to either side. His right hand brushed against something smooth, cold and metallic. He reached frantically with his other hand and gripped his flashlight. Sitting up, he fumbled for the on switch and pushed it forward with his thumb.

Nothing.

The flashlight was broken.

## 6

Fred cradled the flashlight to his chest. His chin quivered. The darkness suddenly felt darker. The cold, colder. He shut his eyes tight and clenched his jaw.

How long would it take for Mr. Howard to begin a search, even if Craig feigned ignorance as to Fred's whereabouts? There was no way they'd leave the river valley without him. But even if the search for him had already started, would they ever find the cave? The entrance itself was almost invisible unless you knew exactly where to look. Craig would have to show them. Unlikely. He would probably play the part of concerned friend and join the search. He might even lead a group up the creek bed canyon, walk within feet of the opening and act as if he'd never seen the place.

Being at the mercy of Craig was the biggest nightmare of all.

Fred suddenly remembered something about the flashlight. Something his dad had shown him years ago. He felt for the base of the metal cylinder, gripped the end and tried to twist it. It didn't budge. He tried again, gritting his teeth in the effort, and this time it moved, if only by a few millimeters. It was hard, the threads likely grimed by years of rust and dirt, but eventually he managed to unscrew the end completely. Three fat batteries tumbled out onto his lap, one of them rolling away into blackness. He tried to stop it, but not before it slipped beyond his fingers.

"Dang it!" he spat and kicked the ground. Things were not going well for him. He returned his attention to the flashlight, specifically the small metal cap he'd just unscrewed. With his fingers he felt for the spiral metal spring and a ring of foam rubber beneath, which he carefully pulled free. When he felt the cold glass bulb wedged in its underside he almost shouted in excitement.

It was precarious work, laboring blind with trembling fingers. But after five minutes he'd replaced the shattered bulb with the new, found the errant battery in the darkness beyond his lap, and returned them all to their proper place. After twisting on the cap, he placed his thumb on the switch.

He hesitated, took a deep breath, and pushed his thumb forward.

Light exploded into the darkness. He fell backward and almost dropped the flashlight a second time. Twin stabs of pain jolted his eyes as they tried to adjust. It was brighter than the sun! More blazing than a nuclear explosion!

The most beautiful thing he'd ever seen.

His wonder wore off quickly. With his blindness healed, he jumped to his feet and swept the beam in a wide circle, three hundred and sixty degrees. The room was indeed enormous, twice the size of a large movie theatre with an even higher ceiling. One side of the room dipped down to a pool of water, doubtless the one he'd fallen into earlier. The opposite side rose slightly upward, increasing in its angle until it was completely vertical where wall met ceiling. It was here he saw a tunnel - the very tunnel he'd fallen from. It was the sloping angle of the rock that had saved his life. Without it, he would have plummeted sixty feet to his death.

Staring at the opening, neck craned back, he placed the tail end of the flashlight in his mouth, keeping the beam trained upon his only known chance of escape, and started forward. His tennis shoes were newish, with rubber soles still treaded deep. Even with wet stone beneath him, he was able to move swiftly up the side of the cave. The tunnel was now only twenty feet above. But the angle was too steep to walk. He leaned forward and let his palms meet rock, then began to crawl. Ten feet from the tunnel, with the slope all but vertical, he began to slide. He bit down hard upon the flashlight and tried to keep from tumbling backward. Once he stopped sliding, he steadied himself, and resumed the climb, this time attempting greater speed. He got closer. But still slid back before reaching the tunnel.

"Really?" he shouted as he slid all the way to the cave floor. His third try brought him closer still to the tunnel, this time within five feet of the tips of his fingers. But to no avail. Enraged, he slid backwards, all the way down. His hands began to blister and swell from their rubbing upon the rough stone. He rested a moment, caught his breath, but kept the beam of his flashlight on the opening above. He could make it. He had to make it. It was only five feet beyond the farthest point he'd reached. Though he was exhausted and in pain, he finally stood up again, stepped back a dozen feet from the incline for a running start, and with a silent, desperate prayer, darted forward like he was running a forty yard dash, zipping past a line of stalagmites, then up, up, up the wall, stretching out his free hand, almost, almost.....but not enough. With a cry of despair, he slid backward to the cave floor.

Three feet. That was all there had between him and freedom. Three feet. His entire body ached now. The exertion had warmed him, but he found he could hardly move. With a defeated sigh he lowered himself to the ground and lay flat. He pulled the flashlight from his mouth and pointed the beam at the tunnel, as if the darkness would erase it the moment he turned away.

Eventually, reluctantly, he turned off the flashlight to conserve energy and bathed himself once again in pitch. When his eyes acclimated to the darkness, he noticed a faint blue glow up above. So faint he wondered if he was imagining things, or hallucinating. But as the minutes passed by, the glow grew slightly brighter as his eyes adjusted more.

"It's daylight!" he said aloud. "It's light creeping down the tunnel."

It wasn't much. But seeing even a hint of the outside world lifted his spirits, if only by a notch. He would rest a while, and then try again. Soon his eyelids drooped, then fluttered, then closed.

Sometime later, waking out of a slumbering haze, Fred heard voices. He sat up straight, rubbed his eyes, and instantly switched on his flashlight, pointing the beam at the tunnel. Mr. Howard was there, holding a rope!

"You alright, powderpuff?" he called down.

"Yes!" Fred cried, standing to his feet. He was too elated to wonder why the man had called him that name. As far as he was concerned, Mr. Howard could call him whatever he liked. He started up the incline as the troop leader began to lower a rope.

"Quite a pickle you're in down there, ain't ya?" Mr. Howard didn't seem the slightest bit disturbed or upset at the situation. Craig had probably not told him what had happened. A cowardly omission soon to be remedied.

When he reached the end of the rope, Fred took hold of it and quickly tied it around his waist. Mr. Howard began to pull him upward, hand over hand.

"You're never gonna believe what happened!" Fred called up as he ascended.

"Oh, I'm sure I will. Craig gave us a full account. He's quite a brash boy, don't ya think?"

By now he was almost to the tunnel, close enough to smell the rubber on Mr. Howard's shoes. But before his head reached the opening, the man stopped pulling. Fred looked up.

"What's wrong?" he asked.

"Oh, nothin'" Mr. Howard said, smiling wide. His white teeth gleamed in the near-darkness. "You just look funny dangling there like a hooked fish. I can see why Craig pushed you overboard. Lame little powderpuff falls like a potato sack!"

Fred's blood went cold. He gripped the rope as tight as he could. "Pull me up!"

"I don't think so," Mr. Howard said. His voice began to change, to get higher, and raspier. His face changed too, popping up with a dozen spontaneous pimples. His thinning brown hair grew thick and curly, and he shrunk a whole foot in an instant. It wasn't Mr. Howard at all.

"Sweet dreams, powderpuff," Craig said and dropped the rope. Fred screamed and fell.

"Nooooo!" he jolted awake, breathless. He was still on the cave floor. It had been a dream. A cruel, terrible nightmare. Looking up to where he thought the tunnel was, he saw no blue glow. It must be night now.

And rescue hadn't come.

# 7

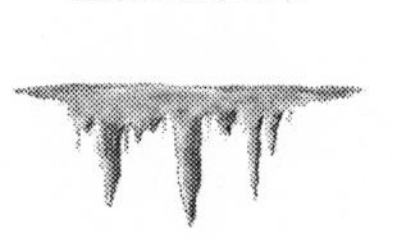

Darkness. Cold. Panic.

A rush of nausea swept over him. He gripped his stomach and tried to steady his breathing, but there was little he could do. His heart pounded erratically against his ribs. His skin felt thick and clammy.

Over twelve hours must have passed now since he'd been pushed, more than enough time for Craig to lead others back. The troop had been scheduled to return to Little Rock that afternoon. He pictured his parents standing in the school parking lot as the van rolled up. They would have been eager to find out how the trip went. If he'd had fun or not. If he'd made friends. But none of that had happened. His mother was sure to be going insane with panic by now, his father trying to hold her together.

"I'm alive," he said between labored breaths, as if they could hear. "I'm alive."

His tongue felt swollen and pasty inside his mouth, and for the first time he realized how thirsty he was. He stood and picked his way across the room, stopping just short of the pool he'd fallen into earlier. The water was shallow for the first several feet, and then deepened to an unknown depth as it neared the far wall. It glowed a deep sapphire in the beam of his flashlight.

He knelt down and dipped his hand into the water, daggers of cold piercing his skin. For a moment he wondered if it was clean. Bacteria could live anywhere. But his thirst was too strong, and overcame any momentary misgivings. He cupped a handful and lifted it to his lips, took an experimental sip. It was sweet. Perfectly clean, as far as he could tell, anyway. He dropped to his belly and lowered his head until his lips met the water's surface. There, he slurped several long draughts until his stomach bulged like a balloon.

Within seconds, his mind cleared as water seeped into his cells. He rose to his feet and swept the flashlight in all directions. The tunnel couldn't be the only way out. In a room that size, there had to be other passages leading somewhere. Whether they went deeper into the cave or toward the outside, he'd have to find out. A cursory examination of nearby walls revealed dozens of shadowed holes and fissures. Some were a farce, dead ends after a foot or two. Others extended deep into the rock. But even the most promising of these eventually tapered off, too narrow for a human to squeeze through. His claustrophobia was also proving a concern. He wondered if he'd have the guts to push through a small tunnel if it so presented itself.

On the far end of the room, the cave floor angled downward, its rock sinking into intermittent patches of mud. He slipped twice before lowering himself into a sitting position and sliding on his rump the rest of the way down. Once he was at the base of the incline, he raised his flashlight to illuminate the looming wall a dozen feet ahead. Where wall met floor, a four-foot hole gaped like an open mouth.

Fred rose to his feet and moved to the opening, crouching low enough to shine his light into its depths. Ten feet in, the passage turned, disappearing behind a corner of stone. He swallowed, licked his lips, and then began to crawl on all fours. It was probably a dead end. Was sure to be. But when he reached the corner and peeked beyond, he could see the tunnel continued onward without shrinking an inch. He glanced back to the mouth of the tunnel, but could see only blackness rimmed with stone. He breathed in, fought the already creeping tendrils of claustrophobia, then continued onward. Three more turns and thirty feet later he found himself staring into another pool. The tunnel had dipped down and was filled three-fourths to the top with water. He could shine his light across the surface and clearly see where the tunnel extended beyond. But it would require swimming with just his head above water. Even the mere thought terrified him. What if he got stuck? What if the water level rose and he drowned?

Dejected, he turned around and made his way back to the main room. Stepping out into the open felt good, though it took five minutes of struggle to climb up the muddy slant. Once at the top he was filthy and aching and bruised and in desperate need for some rest.

"I have to try the main tunnel again," he whispered to himself, though his muscles felt like jelly. When he stood below the rock face, he took one look at the distance from floor to exit and sighed. He had to rest. Just for a little bit. Then he'd try again.

This time, when he lay down, he heard his stomach begin to protest. It gurgled and growled inside him and brought to his mind that he hadn't eaten in over twenty-four hours, longer than he'd gone his entire life. For a while he allowed himself to fantasize about deep-dish pepperoni pizza and mounds of mac and cheese, but the dream without the mouthful was simply torture. It only made his stomach more ornery. He forced all thoughts of food from his mind, turned off his flashlight to conserve the battery, and attempted to sleep again.

With his body shivering, Fred slipped in and out of a half-asleep dream for over an hour before finally drifting off. It was there, in the deep parts of his brain, that he sat before a feasting table with his hands tied behind his back. The smells were intoxicating, turning his mouth into a fountain of saliva. But he could only look on and imagine what it must be like to eat the food. When he finally awoke, half crazy with hunger, he saw at once that the tunnel glowed a faint blue again. It was daylight. The second day. He'd been there for twenty-four hours.

They'll come today, he assured himself. Craig would finally tell them. He'd break down and confess what he'd done. And before long, someone would shine a flashlight from above and see Fred waiting below, covered in mud, shivering from head to toe, but alive.

He tried for the tunnel a few more times, but was dismayed to find he was not improving in his efforts, but getting worse. With no food in his system, his strength was quickly waning. On his third try, he barely made it past the halfway mark. He tripped, smashed his head against the rock and slid back down on his belly. He lay there as if dead and determined to wait until others found him.

Dipping in and out of a fitful sleep, he passed the day until the blue glow faded and night arrived once more. An idea popped into his head and he sat up in search of a shard of rock. When he found a thin sliver of limestone, he picked the flattest spot on a nearby wall and scratched a single notch into the rock to mark the passing of the first day.

Time slipped by in an inky blur. A numbing routine of drinking water from the pool and attempted sleep. Each morning, he scratched another mark into the rock and prayed for rescue, though he began to realize that every passing day made such a prospect more and more unlikely.

Eventually, so tired he could hardly walk, he sank deep into his mind and stayed there, drifting from dream to dream.

He'd been in the cave for three days.

# 8

Sunlight warmed his face. He blinked, opened his eyes. He was standing in the middle of his backyard, crabgrass up to his ankles where his Dad had yet to mow. His tire swing swayed gently beneath their pecan tree, its frayed rope creaking in slow motion. He heard a familiar and beautiful humming and turned to see his mother through the open kitchen window, hunkered over the stove. A hint of frying chicken lingered in the air. His mouth watered.

"Mom?" he called out. She lifted her head and looked out the window, smiling when she saw him. "You make sure you spray bug repellent all over, okay? I couldn't live with myself if you got West Nile."

Her floral sundress rippled in the breeze, as did her hair, rich brown with a touch of gray she refused to color. Fred nodded and waved her off.

"The mosquitos aren't bad today, Mom. Don't worry."

"I always worry, kiddo. It's my job."

He moved to the tire swing and draped his arms over its smoothened treads. "Where's Dad?"

"He'll be home in half an hour. Are you hungry?"

"Yes."

"Good, because I'm working on a feast!"

She retreated back into the kitchen and Fred watched her bustle about for the next several minutes. He'd never really noticed how pretty she was. How she seemed to glide about as if her feet hardly touched the ground. Her mouth was always turned up in a smile. Like she was thinking about some joke. Some funny memory. He could hardly recall her frowning a day of his life. "What a day!" she'd always say, even if it was raining and she was running a fever. His mom was just glad to be alive. To have breath in her lungs and eyes that could see the world.

Fred turned his eyes from the window and looked around him in the backyard. Dappled sunlight riddled the ground like luminous coins, each yellow circle dancing when a breeze rustled overhead branches. He'd never noticed how stunning the color of light was, nor how soothing its warmth. It's not something one thinks about. Not really. But standing there in the yard, he almost felt a hunger for light. He spread his arms wide and tilted his head back, opening himself to the sun like a leaf soaking it in. He closed his eyes, saw yellow fire turned red through his eyelids.

When he opened them again he was not in his back yard.

He was at school, in Biology class. The teacher, Mr. Allen, was drawing the diagram of a plant cell on the chalkboard - mitochondria and organelles rendered in quick, powdery screeches. Most everyone was sleepy after lunch, resting their chins on opened palms, eyes half closed. Fred, however, was all ears, taking fastidious notes. Not so much because he was interested in photosynthesis as much he was with Rebecca Bates. She sat right in front of him, the back of her golden head no more than twenty inches from the tip of his nose, and half that from his fingertips. How many times had he imagined reaching up and running his fingers through those silky tresses? Too many to count. He could smell the fragrance of her strawberry shampoo. Could count the freckles on the back of her neck. There was probably no one else on the planet, including her own parents, who knew that she had precisely 17.5 freckles in the space below and behind her left ear.

He'd hardly said four words strung together to the girl all year. But he was smitten all the same. Not just because of her fragrant locks or freckles either, but because she was smart. The moment Mr. Allen started in on his lessons, she would pull out her glitter unicorn Trapper Keeper and take down his every word in an elegant, bubble letter script. She might be five inches taller than he was, but he didn't care. He'd catch up soon enough when his hormones kicked in. Then, with height and bulging muscles, he'd sweep her off her dainty little feet.

He had a sudden idea. An idea so ambitious, so audacious, he could hardly believe his brain had thought it up. He would write her a note. Simple and to the point. Before he could convince himself otherwise, he reached into his desk and retrieved a sheet of notebook paper and a freshly sharpened number two pencil. He clutched the pencil, bit his tongue, and wrote the first thing that came to mind.

*I like you.*

He folded the paper once, then twice, attending to the corners to make sure they were perfectly crisp right angles. He swallowed, clutched the note and extended his hand until the edge of the paper just rested on her shoulder. She didn't move. Didn't even seem to notice.

And then the bell rang.

She closed her notebook, tucked away her things, and stood up as elegant as a ballerina. Fred closed his fingers around the note and pulled his hand back. He began to gather his own things, averting his eyes. She was out the door before anyone else, instantly decreasing the beauty in the room.

But the air in front of his desk still smelled of strawberry shampoo.

*Next time,* he vowed. *I'll do it next time.*

The scene seemed to ripple, like a stone dropped into a pool. Mr. Allen's classroom shimmered and faded, replaced at once by a mountaintop and a setting sun. His father stood beside him, snapping pictures of dusk as it settled over the Ozark Mountains in a vast amber blaze.

"The sun's falling fast," Fred observed.

"It's actually us that's moving," his father said. "The sun stays put."

When the orange orb touched the horizon, his father snapped pictures all the faster, as if the sun were setting for the last time, never to awaken again. A final sliver of light clung to the edge of the earth and then vanished altogether. His father lowered the camera, took a deep breath, and spoke the words he always did at dusk.

*"I am the light of the world. Whoever follows me will never walk in darkness, but will have the light of life."*

A chilling breeze marked the arrival of night.

Fred's eyes opened and he remembered where he was. The memory of sunlight lingered a moment, then slipped away. He covered his face with his hands and began to sob. Tears ran hot and unabated down his cheeks, his quivering voice moaning in the blackness.

How long could he take this? How much more could he

stand? Trapped in a pit and forgotten. No way out. No way out. Destined to die if he wasn't rescued. He had water. But nothing to eat. His body was already weak and borderline hypothermic. How many days more before he had no strength to move?

Fred's mind ran wild and vivid, painting pictures of his bones years later in the cave, discovered by some spelunker. They'd haul him out in a trash bag, identify him by his dental records and the mystery of his disappearance would finally be solved.

He reached for his flashlight and marking stone and stepped to the cave wall, scraping letters as deep and clear as his remaining strength would allow. When he was done he stared at the message and hoped that someday it would incriminate the guilty to the furthest extent of the law. He might be only bones and hair and crooked teeth by then, but he'd have the final word:

*Craig pushed me.*

# 9

Seven days.

There was little use for movement now. He'd explored as much as he felt he could. With no clear passage out and hardly any energy left in his body, he'd decided to restrict his motions to drinking water from the pool. Other than that, he lay beneath the tunnel, his flashlight clutched to his chest with both hands. Though he loathed the dark, he knew he had to ration what energy the batteries had left. He'd noticed the day before that the beam had grown dimmer. With a week of almost continuous use, this was no surprise, though the rationale behind the knowledge made it no less terrifying. Once or twice a day, he risked a short span of illumination, shining the beam on the tunnel's mouth, though he knew this had no real practical use. It just reminded him that it was there.

Fred felt his mind slipping. Slow at first, almost imperceptible, but then so fast it was impossible to stop. He began to hit the cave floor with his fist, picturing Craig's face there, how he would love to bruise him, hurt him, pummel his nose flat.

"I hate you!" Fred screamed as he pounded the rock. Knives of pain shot up his arm. He bit his lip against a tsunami of rage and cried until his tear ducts were dry.

When he saw the tunnel's faint glow reappear hours later as the seventh day dawned, he realized if he stayed there wallowing, Craig would win. And he couldn't have that. He had to do something. He had to move. He was not dead yet.

The mere act of rising to his feet was an arduous chore. His heart pounded between labored breaths. He felt sluggish, as if he were moving in slow motion. But he was moving now, and that was something. He drank from the pool once more and set out for the far end of the cave.

Once past the muddy slope, he reached the tunnel. It curved round just as he remembered from before, then angled sharply down to the barricade of water. With shoes just touching the pool's edge, he leaned down and shined his flashlight again through the small passage of air, not six inches wide and half that tall, between the water and the roof of the tunnel. There was nothing to see but black, even in the beam of the flashlight. He stood pondering, weighing the options. It was clear the path continued on. Maybe all the way out of the cave, maybe only for a dozen feet before hitting another dead end. Either way, he had to try.

He stepped furtively, one foot into the water, then the other. It was cold, stinging furiously. Thankfully it was not deep at first, only two feet at most. He began to crawl through the water, holding the flashlight above the surface. Where the tunnel started constricting down to the water's surface, he knew he had only one choice. He counted to three and paddled onward until everything was submerged but his face and hands. With one hand he kept the flashlight dry and with the other he pushed himself forward.

The passage continued straight for quite some time, the rock ceiling undulating only by inches above the water. It wasn't long before his teeth began to chatter, followed by a full-bodied shivering so violent that he almost dropped the flashlight. He squeezed the metal handle as hard as he could, feeling his grip would lose all strength within minutes.

There! Up ahead was a flash of light. What was it? He narrowed his eyes to focus. There were dozens of pinpricks. Like quartz deposits in the rock, facets reflecting back the flashlight's beam. No. Not quartz.

They were moving.

Fred froze. The specks of light were sliding up and down the walls and clinging to the ceiling. There was no way to continue without pushing through them. They were obviously some kind of cave creature. Spiders? Pale and blind and possibly poisonous.

He couldn't move now, frozen by more than cold. The mere idea of hairy legs and exoskeletons was enough to make him want to head right back from where he had come. His breathing quickened to staccato gasps. His heart raced. He couldn't do this. He couldn't do this.

*Don't do it and you will die.*

The voice in his head was right, though he took no comfort from the fact. What good was it to live if he was forced to wade through a tangle of insects that might bite and sting and send him into anaphylactic shock?

*You must go.*

He squinted his eyes shut and crawled forward. In seconds, he felt the first creature clinging to his head. He reached up and tore it free, but did not stop. Then came another, and another, and another until he could no longer remove them all. The moment he could pull at one, three other replaced it. They were large bugs with long thin legs and flailing antennae, and now they were all over him - his hair, his face, his neck, his hand. They made a kind of faint screeching sound as they jumped, their shelled bodies smashing into the rock with hollow thumps. Fred let out an unbridled scream of horror and rushed forward as fast as his knees and single hand would take him. Twice his head struck against low hanging rock, but the bugs hung on like a living garment. He saw stars through his closed eyelids, felt himself on the verge of passing out from cold and terror. But then the floor began to rise along with the ceiling. The water level sank and sank around his quaking body until he found himself crawling and dripping onto dry rock once again.

The pool was behind him.

Still frantic, he slapped at his face and head until the bugs were all knocked free or crushed. When he opened his eyes and shined his flashlight upon the carnage, he saw they were crickets - cave crickets - white as bone with ink black eyes and legs like jointed straw. He shivered in disgust, then straightened up and walked on as fast as his hypothermic body would allow.

The passage had narrowed here, but not so much as to block his progress. With heavy breaths he lumbered up the path. It began to ascend. He felt a gust of warmer air.

*This is it! This is the way out!*

He rounded a bend in the rock and instantly saw the most beautiful sight he had ever seen: sunlight! Luscious, gleaming sunlight cutting down into the dark. In less than twenty feet he would be out in the open, alive and free. He could already smell growing things, the sharp tinge of pine, the sweet scent of honeysuckle.

Something jarred his shoulder. He twisted sideways as a blast of pain shot down his right side and he fell, sprawling.

He was facedown on the rock floor, wedged sideways at the base of the passage. It was too narrow here for him to proceed facing forward. It took a bit of shimmying and squirming but he managed to get on his feet again, this time facing sideways into the tunnel ahead. He stepped forward more carefully this time, and as he did, he moved full on into a ray of sunlight. For a moment he didn't move. Just let the beams warm his skin. He inhaled fresh forest air through his nose, reveling in the green smell, and then commenced his ascent.

But he was stopped again. The walls had drawn too close together. He turned completely sideways and managed four more feet, but even then, with the walls allowing only a few inches to pass through he could not take another step. He tried. Hard. In a frantic stretch of arms and legs and fingers. But pushing any further was to risk getting permanently stuck. Finally, scraped and exhausted, he stopped, resting his forehead on the wall.

Birds flittered from branch to branch only a dozen unreachable feet away, talking to one another in song. He could see the sky outside, smell the lush green of leaves, all through a narrow gap that was now nothing more than a prison window. Fred pressed his hands against his temples and gritted his teeth. The sound was a soothing torture.

So close to freedom.

But still chained fast to the world of shadows.

He stood there and wept until the sun was gone.

## 10

He'd forgotten just how loud the woods got when the sun went down--cicadas filling the evening air with their harsh vibrations, as if they were growling at the stars. Parts of the cave were padded with a layer of moss where sunlight could reach across the stone floor. He ran his hand over the green carpet, thankful for such texture after days of only cold, hard rock. When his legs grew too weak to stand, he inched down and lay on his side, tearing a large wad of moss to clump together beneath his head for a pillow. Comforted by the balmy summer air, he closed his eyes and let exhaustion take him.

He was awakened by a raccoon that had come sniffing and rustling into the cleft. Fred's odor--the result of a week without bathing--was probably strong enough to draw anything with a nose. He must smell like something decaying to the little beast. It came within two feet of his head before he jumped up and shouted it away. The raccoon hissed, equally startled, and retreated frantically from the mouth of the cave.

Outside, the sky was just brightening, flecks of red on a

line of clouds beyond the trees. It was morning again. The eighth day.

He thought hard on what to do. Without carving away at the stone walls on either side of the opening, there would be no way out. At its smallest point, the passage was only three inches wide. He tried tapping at the rock with the butt end of the flashlight but this hardly made a dent. He sat still as day arrived. The air outside warmed, sitting humid and heavy on his skin.

By midday, he pondered his weakness, and his gnawing hunger. He felt his body devouring itself. Soon he would not be able to move, or even cry for help. There had to be a trail running outside somewhere near the fissure. Some offshoot from the main trail along the river. There were many hikers this time of year, groups of climbers, families out picnicking. There could be dozens of people within earshot at that very moment.

"Help!" he cried, and then much louder. "Help! Help me!"

The sound of his voice echoed in the cleft, reflected and magnified by the rock like a giant stone megaphone. He shouted even louder, waited for an answer, and then shouted louder still. For hours he persisted, until his throat felt shredded and his voice was all but gone. When the sun sank toward dusk again he settled on the floor, delirious with fatigue.

"Help..." he croaked in a raspy whisper. His chin quivered, but he had no tears to cry. Without a drink in over a day, he was dehydrated and getting worse by the hour. To get a drink, he knew he had to move back into the cave where crickets stood guard over the flooded tunnel. He loathed the idea, but his thirst was stronger, and it won out.

They seemed even more numerous than he remembered. At one point, there was no glimpse at all of rock, every inch covered by an undulating tangle of legs and antennae. His feet crunched on dozens as he approached the water, despite his efforts to kick them out of the way. They leapt and clung to his skin, hair, and clothing. Once at the water's edge, he knelt down and sucked up a bellyful of water. The cave crickets all but swarmed him, a thousand sticky legs holding tight to his skin. When he had his fill, he turned and fled back toward the fissure, slapping furiously at the creatures as he went. Once he was at the barricade, he stopped and removed every cricket he could find, flinging them down into the darkness. When they were gone, he collapsed and covered his face with his hands.

The water had served to clear his head, but he still spent the rest of the day trying to ignore his hunger. It had become a living force, like his stomach had taken control of his head. There were no more fantasies of burgers and pizza. Now there was only a single minded, laser-focused lust for anything edible. Anything.

At a certain point in the day, when the sun shined upon the moss just so, its green grew luscious in his eyes. He'd never been much for salads, or vegetables in general, but the tiny green velvet seemed to call to him. He tore a small piece free, sniffed it, found it earthy and somewhat sweet. Then, almost before he realized what he was doing, he stuffed it in his mouth and began to chew.

Sand and grit crunched hard between teeth. The moss seemed more dirt than plant. He tried to swallow, but found a wad of clay and earth sticking to the back of his throat. He coughed and spat until his mouth was clear, scraping his tongue with his fingers to remove any vestige of the unseemly snack. Eating moss would take a more delicate hand, it seemed. He picked at another mound, retrieving only pinches of velvet green between his fingers. Though these proved edible enough, they were more a culinary tease than an adequate source of nourishment. It would take him days to gather enough for even a decent meal. And still there was the question of whether the moss would end up making him sick. In the end, he settled on waiting. He sat down and stared out at the daylight.

He wondered if this was what it felt like to be in prison, barred off from the outside world. Or solitary confinement, denied interaction with another living soul. Fred was beginning to understand the torture of such methods. Humans were made to converse, to share moments and words. Even the most solitary of introverts needed this to survive, or at least to maintain sanity. He'd been in the cave for eight days. He knew there were prisoners who had spent lifetimes in a concrete box without so much as a word whispered under the door.

But at least they had been fed.

Even prison food sounded gourmet at the moment. What he wouldn't give for a stale piece of bread and stinky cheese! What he wouldn't give for anything at all. His stomach continued to chide him, writhing within his gut like a rope twisting upon itself. He had to eat. He had to.

Something jumped over his shoulder from behind and landed right in front of him. He looked down and saw a cave cricket crouched with legs poised for another jump. Something clicked and he suddenly forgot his loathing of the creatures and began to salivate. His stomach churned. How many cultures ate bugs as a normal part of their diet? What was the big deal?

No sooner did these arguments pass rapidly through his starving brain then he shot out his hand and snatched up the critter before it could escape. He lifted it to his face as its limbs writhed in vain. He closed his eyes, and thrust it in his mouth, chewing instantly. It squished and crunched and turned to mush between his teeth. He swallowed and clamped a hand over his mouth, expecting to throw up at any second. But his stomach seemed to take the snack easily enough. And as he thought of it, the creature hadn't tasted all that bad. Its texture left something to be desired. But its flavor was somewhat sweet, almost like a mushroom, with hints of bitterness not unlike certain cheeses he'd tried before.

He stood up and moved back into the cave where the creatures clung to rock in limitless supply. He plucked another one free, popped it in his mouth, chewed, and swallowed. The second one was even better.

When his stomach realized it was finally being fed, it seemed to take immediate control of his body. He lost all sense of timidity, dropped to all fours, and began to shovel the writhing insects into his mouth, chewing and swallowing as fast as he could. Ten minutes later, he was so full he could hardly move. He drank a mouthful of water to swish out bits of leg and antennae from his teeth and crawled back to daylight for a nap, satiated from his unexpected feast.

# 11

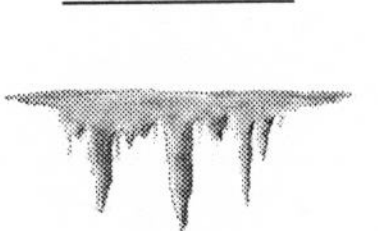

The crickets proved a valuable source of energy. Within hours, he felt his strength returning. For a while, time passed in a series of mundane periods of eating and drinking and waiting and thinking. There was the problem of where to relieve himself without contaminating his water or food supply, but once he found a small offshoot on the near side of the water and established it as his subterranean latrine, he was able to settle into a seemingly indefinite routine. With the warmth of the air, the smell of his waste became hard to endure in that enclosed space, but at least he was near the surface, where the occasional gust of fresh air diminished the stench. Of course there were the flies. Drawn to the odor, they soon began to swarm inside the fissure. Fred tried his best to ignore them, but they proved to be quite a nuisance.

Much of his time was spent devising a new plan of escape. All of the surrounding rock was limestone, and though not as soft as sandstone, he knew he could scrape it away with the handle of the flashlight without damaging the bulb or the wiring. The question was, which would wear away first, metal or stone? He crouched on his knees and peered forward through the fissure. Ten feet to freedom. That was all. He could focus on widening the bottom portion to allow him to squeeze through on his belly. It would take a long time. But what else could he do?

With his expectations high, he took the flashlight and turned it backward in his hand. He placed it at an angle against the rock and slowly began to push it back and forth, back and forth, pressing harder with each stroke. The good news was that the metal surface managed to cut away an almost inch-long swath in the wall, measuring a centimeter deep. The bad news was that it took almost an hour do so. When he finished this first experiment and set the flashlight down, his arms felt almost useless. He stared at the rock, trying to calculate just how long it would take to carve his way out. Even if he possessed superhuman strength and worked nonstop round the clock, it would take over ten days. Considering his need to rest, not to mention sleep, the task would take three times as long. This put him trapped in the cave for well over a month.

A month.

The realization bombarded him with a wave of gloom. He lowered his head and rested it on his open palm. Could he survive that long? Even if there remained plenty to eat and drink, would his mind hold up? Could he possibly stay sane? There was no way to know. The reality of what it would take to return to the world of sky and sun and people was so daunting he could do little but breathe.

Nevertheless, the next morning, after breakfasting on a handful of crickets, he began. The flashlight felt good in his hands, the cold metal warming quickly against his palm. With shoulders hunched for leverage, he pushed back and forth as hard as he could. Rock crumbled and fell almost at once. He smiled. It would work. It had to work. By midday he had managed to widen half a foot of stone by an inch. He allowed himself a bit of rest and stared at what he'd accomplished. Part of him was elated that the job was possible. The rock would give way, eventually. But another side of his mind pondered just how weak he felt, how the morning's work had seemed like many days compressed into one. His arms did not just ache. They were on fire. All the way down to the bone. He stretched his fingers in attempt to push out the pain. They felt as raw as ten bloated sausages attached to his palm. But he had no choice but to press on.

Something cawed outside in the open. Fred looked up.

A coal-black crow sat perched on a tree just beyond the fissure, tilting its head back and forth as if studying him. Fred blinked. Waited for it to go away. But it remained there, observing his every move.

Fred sighed with irritation. "Go away," he muttered at it. But the crow did not obey.

Hours later, beyond exhausted, he held the flashlight in weakened hands and closed his eyes. He knew he needed to rest, if only for a moment.

*What is the use?* A voice spoke from outside.

Fred's eyes flew open. The crow was still watching him.

*I asked you a question, child. What is the use of what you do there?*

Fred froze, peering into the doll's eye gaze of the creature. It was a dozen yards away, but its voice was clear inside his head. He decided he must be dreaming.

"I am carving my way out of here," he said.

The bird chuckled, but the sound was more like sand ground between teeth. It shook its greasy plumage, gave three quick beats of its wings, and leapt down to the entrance of the cave. It stuck its beak into the shadows and stared at the boy all the harder. *Why labor for something impossible? There is no way out.*

"I disagree."

*But you will die of exhaustion before you succeed.*

"I have no other choice."

*Of course you do!* The crow laughed again. Fred wished it would stop finding his fate amusing.

"Leave me alone," he said.

*I most certainly will not. I am your only friend. I am the first voice you have heard since you fell, am I not?*

"You're not real."

*How do you know?*

"Because crows don't talk."

In response, the bird drew in its wings and stepped fully into the cave. In four quick hops it was almost upon him, but stopped within arm's length.

*I am no figment of your fevered imagination,* it said proudly. *If that's what you're thinking.*

"Yes you are! You're a hallucination. And I wish you'd go away."

The crow cawed softly, as if offended.

"Why are you here?" Fred asked.

*I've come to save you from believing in things unattainable. Why leap when the sky is so high? Why swim when you will only drown? Stay safe, I say. Stay safe where risk cannot reach you, and neither can pain.*

Fred scraped harder still. Rock crumbled and fell. "Are you suggesting I remain here? That I actually stay in the cave?"

*Why not? There is everything you could possibly need. It is not bereft of discomforts, to be sure. But life is not a party, child. It is survival. It is digging in where the ground is soft enough and staying put. It is thanking your lucky stars when you have a meal to eat, be it carrots or crickets. It is being content.*

"I could never be content here."

*Why?*

"I want to see the sun."

The crow glanced over its shoulder at the growing day, then looked back at Fred. *You can see the sun well enough already.*

"But I want to feel it."

*Trust me, you are much safer in the dark. The light reveals too many things better left hidden.*

"You're a liar!" he spat.

The crow leaned down even closer as Fred scraped. It brought its onyx beak within an inch of the other's ear and spoke almost in a hiss. *I know what you endure, child. I know the way others look at you when you enter a room. They laugh at the mere sight of you! You are a strange, sad sort of creature. So smart that people hate you. So awkward that folks will never stop gawking at how you walk, how you speak, even how you raise your hand. They will laugh at you forever and always. Mark my words.*

"It's not like that."

*Indeed, child, it's worse. Mind your hands.*

Fred looked down and saw drops of blood sprinkled on the ground. He pulled one hand from the flashlight, then the other and turned them over to examine. Both palms were almost entirely blistered. Somehow, in the adrenalin of his discussion with the crow, he hadn't felt the onslaught of increasing discomfort. But looking now on the bulbous pockets of fluid, many of them burst and bleeding, a jolt of pain flashed up both arms. It felt like his hands had been dipped in acid or boiling water until the skin had sloughed away.

*My poor, poor child,* the crow said. *How maddening it must be to fail.*

“What am I going to do?” Fred asked, holding his palms upward as they burned.

*Rest,* the crow counseled. *And do not try again.*

# 12

His hands were worse the next morning, swollen and oozing. It was torturous even to move his fingers. He sat on the rock floor and stared at the morning light as it danced through leaves and branches. He closed his eyes and breathed deep, imagining himself out in the open, arms flung wide, with no shadows or walls to keep him prisoner.

There was nothing he could do. In maddening despair, he lay flat on his back and draped his arm over his eyes. When flies landed on his blistered hands he shook them wildly, though the effort caused fresh waves of fiery pain. He tried hard to hold it together, but his chin began to quiver as fresh tears rolled down. He had no choice but to stay there, to wait until his hands were healed enough to resume the scraping. He decided to use shreds of his shirt in the future as a makeshift glove to ensure no more blisters. He would learn from his mistakes. He would work as long and as hard as he could to escape into freedom. He would not listen to the crow.

*Sleep,* he told himself. *Close your eyes and forget everything until your hands are healed.*

He breathed a long and weary sigh and closed his eyes. Despite the pain, he managed to sink into a sleep so deep the world became vapor.

ICY WIND CLAWED at his face. The sun was shining outside the cave, no longer the yellowish glow of summer, but pale and white and faded. The leaves were gone from the trees, exposing craggy gray branches and limbs trembling in the cold. Snow was on the ground now, blown round in powdery clouds that sparkled in weakened sunlight.

Fred tried to move but could not. He was on his stomach in the fissure. He felt one arm stretched forward, his fingers still clutching the flashlight. He knew he had carved many feet of rock, closer than ever to the opening of the cave. But he was so tired now. It had taken so long. There was no counting days. Or even weeks. Now seasons marked the passage of time. Summer had given way to autumn, autumn to winter. He was so close. So close. Only days away. If only he could manage to lift the flashlight. Fred clenched his teeth. They felt brittle and exposed. He looked down at his arm. There on the cave floor, where his hand should have been were only bones, white and bare, picked clean of flesh. Still clutched within a skeleton's fingers was the flashlight, worn now to a stub of shredded metal.

He tried to scream, but had no lungs, only an empty rib cage.

*You're much better now,* someone croaked. He turned his eyes to see the Crow perched upon his shoulder blade. It leaned its head down and pecked the final piece of desiccated flesh from his neck, chewing and swallowing in an instant.

Fred awoke screaming. The light was gone but the air was warm and he could hear wind rustling leaves outside the cave. His heart rate slowed down. It had been just a dream, after all.

Or an omen.

He could not sleep the rest of the night, staring up into the dark. His hands were so tender even the caress of the wind hurt them. But to shield them from the elements was to risk touching them, and that would hurt worse than anything. He held them palm up on his thighs and pondered what to do next.

He was certain now that the dream had showed him what awaited if he stayed there. He would die. The torture of seeing unreachable sunlight would eventually destroy his soul. Winter would come and freeze his bones.

It took two more days for his hands to scab over and harden enough for movement. He ate as many crickets as he could, then stuffed his pockets full. He checked the flashlight and found the beam still strong, then crept slowly back down into the flooded tunnel. The water's cold stole his breath away but he continued onward until all but the top half of his head was submerged. Holding the flashlight above water as before he passed quickly through the tunnel and reached the other side within minutes. He climbed out of the water, shook himself as dry as possible, and continued on to the main room. The wider space, though darker than dark, served to calm him in a way. At least there he didn't have to stare at something he could never reach. At least there he could try to find another way.

His first effort was to retry the main tunnel above, from where he'd been pushed into this dark world. He was lighter now, and had fresh energy from the crickets. Perhaps he could conquer that final three feet that had barred him before. After clambering up the muddy slope he made his way easily to the far side of the cave that had been his dark home for those first terrifying days. He shined the flashlight at the tunnel. It looked closer now. Lower. Reachable.

After several deep breaths, he crouched low, counted to three, and sprang forward at a sprint. He reached the base of the incline, bounded up like a mountain goat. To his shock, his hands were able to reach and grip the bottom lip of the tunnel. He hung there, legs kicking wildly over a sheer drop beneath. For a moment of pure elation he thought he might be able to pull himself up, but the sudden overwhelming pain from his scabbed blisters and the weight of his body loosed his grip and yanked him downward once again. He lowered his arm to catch himself, smashed against the rock, heard and felt a snap, then rolled all the way down. When he reached the bottom at last, he tried to rise, but white-hot pain consumed his upper arm, like someone had stabbed him with a knife and twisted it. He grimaced, cried out, almost fainted. A dull numbness now pooled within the tissue. He reached over with his other arm to feel for an injury, probing fingers immediately feeling and withdrawing from an unnatural shard of bone jutting out from within his arm. He gingerly tried to move it, but fresh pain flashed him to nausea.

His arm was broken.

The realization settled upon him like an anvil on his chest. The blisters were a nuisance. But a broken bone was a death sentence. He would not be able to climb out. Nor would he be able to carve his way out with only one good arm. His only two options for escape had just been utterly and irretrievably torn from his grasp.

He was going to die there.

Fred lay motionless for a long while. He thought of his parents, tried to imagine their faces but saw only their twisted contortions of grief. How long would it take to meet his end? How long could he survive on crickets alone? How could he end things quickly, so he would not have to suffer?

No. He could not, would not think this way.

He struggled to his feet and moved to the larger pool for a drink. Reaching the water's edge was much harder now, but with a series of groans and grunts he was able to lean down enough to scoop out a handful of water and bring it to his lips. Once he'd had his fill he sat down with the flash-light on his legs, its beam shining into the aqua depths of the pool. He soon noticed something odd about its far edge, where cave wall met the water, deep under its surface. There seemed a blacker emptiness there, as if another tunnel lay submerged.

Maybe there was another way out after all.

# 13

Doubts struck almost immediately. If in fact there was a tunnel beneath the pool, the only way forward was completely underwater. He'd never been a strong swimmer. Disliked it even on a warm day in the sun. He'd be swimming blind, holding his breath, all but frozen to the bone. And what of his flashlight? Even if he ended up feeling his way to another room, the thing would be waterlogged - batteries, bulb, wiring and all. He could try to dry it out after the fact, but there was always the risk that his light would be gone forever.

Fred switched off the beam. Its battery life felt more precious than ever. There in shrouded silence his mind raced, distracting him from a barrage of pain in his blistered hand, his broken arm, his every weary cell. Voices spoke to him in the dark.

*You mustn't risk it,* the Crow said. *You know that you cannot swim well. You will drown within seconds. It is far too cold. You will perish from hypothermia. Your light will go out. The mere notion is insanity. You mustn't even think of it.*

The sound of the bird's voice, though grating, offered a

kind of comfort. It concurred with thoughts he'd already had. There was no lie in them. Each warning was sound.

And then another voice came. This one was quieter. No rasp or croak. Just soothingly steady words echoing inside his head like memories.

A voice that sounded like his dad's voice.

*You must go deeper to get free.*

"But I might die," Fred countered.

*You will surely die if you stay. You might live if you go.*

"It's too risky."

*Risk is the only way to live.*

Fred thought on this a moment. All the stories in all of history had said the same. No hero becomes such through playing it safe. By taking the easy, common road. They find their victories by risking it all. By diving in, full bore, aware that failure might take them in the end. But reading a story is much different than standing on the precipice yourself.

"I'm afraid."

*Have courage, you are not alone.*

Fred stood to his feet and switched on the light. Darkness fled from its beam. He took a step toward the water, then stopped. The Crow's voice did not hesitate to speak.

*Do not imagine yourself immortal. You are not. Your pride will kill you. Wait here for the chance of rescue.*

Fred shut his eyes, clenched his fists. He just wanted to do the right thing. The wise thing. Which was it? Going or staying?

*It is wise to stay,* the Crow said.

The other voice spoke at once. *Do not let fear masquerade as wisdom.*

He stepped closer still to the water.

*It is suicide,* the Crow was hissing now.

But Fred did not need to hear another word. His decision was made. He took the final step into the water and hardly felt its frigid sting as he lumbered forward. The floor of the pool angled downward inch by inch, then foot by foot until he was all but underwater. With his toes just barely touching submerged rock, he reached the far wall. His face was above water, his flashlight held high with one arm, its beam sweeping erratic in the air as he tried to stay afloat. With his feet, he probed for the submerged tunnel. It was easy to find, much wider than any tunnel he'd moved through. At least he would not get trapped. Not at first.

His body shook violently now. The cold was already taking him, seeping into his bones. It was now or never. With his thumb, he turned off the flashlight and dove underwater. Within seconds, his head crunched against the roof of the tunnel. He saw stars in the dark, felt a swirl of dizziness, but kept on swimming as hard as he could. There was no way to tell if he was heading in the right direction, or which way he was facing. He was swimming in icy tar, every muscle growing sluggish in the cold. His lungs began to burn. Panic followed quickly. He had no idea how much time had passed, nor how far he had come. But he soon knew that only seconds remained before he passed out. His mind was already dimming. The next moment his legs grew too weak to move. One and then the other became rigid as wood. He could only paddle with one hand now, but even this felt no stronger than a twig.

And then his body went rigid, slipping into final shutdown. Bubbles leaked from his mouth, gurgled upward in the water. Slowly he sank, one foot, two feet, until his bent knees struck smooth rock below. His burning lungs turned to fire and his mind filled with ropes of fog. His thoughts spun and swirled and twisted, then faded one by one by one like lights going out in a darkened house, until all that he saw was the face of his mother and father, smiling in the sun, waiting for him to join them in the warmth.

His body no longer moved, just floating and bobbing gently in the cold dark.

Then, the second before his lungs gave way in surrender to the water trying to kill him, his legs kicked in one final lurch and shot him upward like a torpedo. His sluggish mind expected his head would crunch against rock, but there was no rock to strike. He broke the water's surface in a fantastic splash, gulping instinctively for air. New life surged into his frame and he half-swam, half-splashed hard toward some hoped-for shore. It arrived in seconds, a smooth lip of stone that allowed him to roll out of the water with the last of his energy. He collapsed on his back, gasping and coughing and grateful to be alive.

When his shivering finally subsided and his teeth relented from their chattering, he remembered his flash-light. Had it survived as he had? He lifted it to his face, allowing the water to drain. For the next several minutes he carefully removed the batteries, dried them, blew into the empty cavity to dry it as well, then reassembled everything in the dark.

"Please God," he whispered, then threw the switch. Nothing happened. He turned it off, then on again. It flick-ered feebly, and then went out. He turned it off once more, waited a moment, shook it hard to remove all residual mois-ture, then tried again. This time the beam returned deli-ciously bright. Fred shouted in joy and kissed the glass face as it glowed warm against his lips.

# 14

When Fred swept his light throughout the new room, his breath caught in his throat. It was smaller than the first, but every space was filled with cave formations of the most exquisite shape and color. Where the first room had been drab and virtually monochrome with variant shades of brown, this one was adorned from wall to wall with blues and reds and ambers, as if some hermit artist had encrusted it with gems.

He remembered the cave book he'd read the year before and the pictures on its pages. It had listed every known cave formation in exhaustive detail. Many of them were here: Stalactites hanging from the ceiling like icicles of yellow cream. Mounds of flowstone billowing from the walls. Much of the ceiling was spiked with soda straws, the tiny siblings of stalagmites and there was cave popcorn dotting many surfaces like barnacles on the hull of a ship. Fred even spotted a bit of cave bacon here and there. No more edible than a sliver of rock, of course, but so identical in appearance to the breakfast meat that his mouth watered torturously.

*Beautiful,* he thought. *Utterly, stunningly beautiful.*

When the adrenalin of his underwater venture began to fade, his knees threatened to buckle beneath him. He had to sit down, at least for a while.

How ironic this room had been here the whole time, its beauty hidden behind a simple shroud of water. True, he'd almost died getting there. How easily he could have drowned in the dark. The fact that breath still filled and refilled his lungs seemed a miracle. He'd never so much as pondered the luxury of air. Now it felt sweet and cool in his chest, a gift with every inhalation. Even more, he'd faced his fears. He'd taken the dive. And the stunning sight before him now felt like a gift. A hopeful omen.

His eyes welled with tears, warm lines of salt flowing down his already sodden cheeks. But they fell not from fear or pain or self-pity. They were distilled from joy, a joy as small as a mustard seed, but joy all the same. The first happy tears he'd ever cried in his miserable life.

"Thank you," he whispered to the air, to the voice, to his father who had seemed to speak to him from a million miles away, saving his life.

Then the moment passed, and his tears ceased.

He had not come there to marvel over beauty, but to find a way of escape.

It was time to get moving.

He picked his way along the outer rim of the room and quickly found a passage that corkscrewed down into darkness. The tunnel was wider than it was tall and he would have to crawl on all fours to transverse it. At least there was no water in it, though. For that he was thankful. He sank to his knees and shined the flashlight into the opening. After a final glance over his shoulder, he turned and descended into the passage. His pace was swift, emboldened by the earlier risk he'd taken that had paid off.

Now, the tunnel dipped sharply downward. He gripped the walls as best he could, though his broken bone gnawed and cut with every move. His hand felt numb and useless. Still, he refused to slow, progressing by inches until the angle leveled off. But now the ceiling was even lower. Just tall enough for him to squeeze through on his belly. It was not so much of a problem at first. Not until he saw the bat.

It was gray and furry, clinging upside down to the ceiling with tiny clawed feet. Fred froze and kept his light steady on the critter. The cave book had had an entire chapter on bats. Different species, diet, social patterns, as well as the myriad of diseases they potentially carried. But only one disease sprang up in his mind as being particularly terrifying.

Rabies.

Bats carried the scourge as commonly as any mammal on the planet. And they didn't even have to bite you to give it. One measly drop of their saliva was enough. Before you know it you were foaming at the mouth, and going all batty. Fred had seen the movie Old Yeller far too many times to ignore the risk. With no more than an inch or two of wiggle room on either side of the creature, Fred would find little protection if he tried to slip by. But again, what else was he supposed to do? This was the only way.

He swallowed, muttered a prayer of protection, and moved forward as carefully as he could. Pressed as close to the wall as possible he found himself face to face with the bat. The creature took no notice of him, apparently asleep. Up close, it looked no less creepy. Its face was a cluster of leathery translucence, nose and mouth and eyes squeezed together as if crushed by some tiny invisible fist. Its chest pulsated with quick spurts of breath. He could just see the tip of a single fang protruding from under its upper lip. It was a brown bat, *eptesicus fuscus*, a feaster on moths and wasps and beetles. It was also endangered, though Fred felt no compassion for the creature as he inched past. He tried hard to limit unnecessary movement so as not to wake it, even slowed his breathing, though his head grew dizzy with the effort. He imagined what the bat could do if startled, flapping about wildly and biting him in a flurried rage.

Right when it seemed he had successfully moved beyond the creature, the very tip of his right foot barely brushed against its fur. Instantly his fears were realized. The bat released its grip from the ceiling and began to fly in frantic circles. Every leathery beat of its wings brushed against him. He shielded his face with his hands and tried not to shriek, and within seconds the creature was gone. He looked up just in time to see it disappear down the tunnel. It had not been as keen on attacking him as it had been on escape.

*Escape.*

The bat knew the way out.

That sudden epiphany drove him faster, though the tunnel grew smaller. At one point he felt the familiar dread of being trapped like in the fissure, rock pressing in from all sides with nowhere to go. But then, before the claustrophobia took over, the tunnel began to widen. Soon he was able to crawl, then crouch, then stand. By then, the tunnel was as big as any he had found before. When it began to ascend, he felt a jolt of elation. A gust of wind swept down the corridor and rustled his hair. It was fresh and humid.

*I'm almost free,* his mind cried. *It's almost over.*

But a minute later, the path leveled off and began to meander right and left like a gigantic worm's tunnel. When it dipped down and resumed its descent Fred fought an onslaught of dread. What if it kept on going down and down and down? What if it dead-ended? No, he'd felt the wind. And the bat had to have gone somewhere.

Right as this thought crossed his brain, the tunnel opened up into another room, the floor disappearing in a sheer drop. He froze, steadied himself on the tunnel walls. For a moment, he wondered if he'd managed to unknowingly find his way back to the first tunnel, to the very spot where Craig had pushed him. But the notion was instantly dashed when he noticed how different this new room was. There were more stalactites hanging from the ceiling and no pool on the far side of the chamber. The drop-off was different as well, steeper, with an additional dozen feet or so from ledge to floor. He lowered to his knees and stared down the vertical rock face. How he would manage to get down there was beyond him.

Another gust of air moved past, warmer than normal, smelling of trees. He had to be close.

There came a strange sound from somewhere beyond his flashlight's beam. It was distant, but clear. When it faded he wondered if his imagination was playing tricks. But seconds later it happened again.

Moaning. Moaning in the dark.

# 15

Without taking time to think, Fred dropped to the floor of the tunnel and switched off his flashlight. In the darkness, he listened. But all was silent now. A silence so dense it seemed the very air was thickened by shadow. Some creature out there had made the sound. A sad, mournful cry. Almost human. The idea was both glorious and terrifying.

The sound came again, soft at first, almost imperceptible, then building to a crescendo as if the creature was being tortured in some deep down chamber. Fred fought the urge to cover his ears. He started to slink backward in the tunnel, finding it nearly impossible to proceed.

Still, when the sound faded a second time, he stopped his retreat and thought hard on this new obstacle. Whatever it was (and his imagination could conjure up a myriad of nasty possibilities) it stood between captivity and freedom. Why let a mere sound divert him? After coming so far. Enduring so long. Having braved black water and injury, he stood there not from chance, but from courage, however minute. No. He would move on and face the sound, though he was nauseous with fear.

He switched on his flashlight and examined the space just beyond the tunnel. To the right of the its mouth, he discovered an extension of stone just six inches wide descending at a gradual angle along the wall to the floor below. If he was careful, he might be able to inch along the shelf with his back pressed against rock. At the highest point, it was easily fifty feet from floor to ledge, enough to kill him if he slipped and fell to the bottom. His nerves had betrayed him at a fraction of such a height on the bluff so many days ago. And that fall had only bruised him.

His body trembled as he inched toward the ledge. He tried to calm his mind with simple facts: The bat had flown this way. He'd felt the gusts of air. He was still on the right track.

Fears snapped at him like a circle of angry dogs but he forced them down and prepared to step out upon the ledge. With flashlight clutched in his right hand he took the first sideward step, mindful to keep his weight toward his back. With eyes fixed upon his feet, he moved along steadily, step by careful step. Twice he stopped to catch his balance where the ledge grew thin or the wall bulged outward. But ever onward and downward he moved until his feet touched level ground. There, he dropped to his knees in trembling relief.

The moaning resumed as if on cue, cutting short his celebration. Though blood chilled in his veins, he jumped to his feet and raised his light in the direction of the sound. The room was longer than it was wide, and curved round in a gentle crescent, hiding from his eyes what awaited round the bend.

"You will not stop me," Fred said. He swallowed, took several deep breaths, and then started forward. The moaning grew louder as he drew near. He faltered. Just a few more steps would bring him in contact with its source.

Curiosity and horror mingled in his head, spinning in tandem, driving him mad. What could be down here, so deep in the earth? He took another step, then another, then another, until the sound faded once again. When it did he paused, held the flashlight firm in both hands, pressed his cheek against the warmth of its glass face, and closed his eyes.

All he wanted was to speak to his parents, to somehow send his thoughts through all this rock and dirt and roots of trees. To tell them he was okay, even if he wasn't. To somehow comfort their tortured minds. How long had it been since he'd heard his mother's voice or felt his father's crushing embrace? He'd stopped notching days upon rock long ago. And in his dark prison, every day felt like an aeon of time.

His head began to spin, crippling vertigo rising without warning. He wavered, then eased himself to the ground where he lay on his side, curled around the flashlight's warm illumination. Bit by bit, the dizziness faded until he could lie there without feeling the room was spinning like a top.

Thankfully, the phantom moaning sound had not returned even after several minutes. Perhaps whatever had made it was gone altogether. He knew either way, he must sleep for now. The flashlight's beam shown pale red through his closed eyelids and he felt a rush of gratitude for such a simple thing. He could not have come this far without the light. The little metal cylinder had saved his life, more than once. He clutched it tighter and drifted off to sleep.

The dreams came at once, almost as if they'd been waiting him out, waiting for him to return to their world.

He stood in a brightly lit corridor, the ceiling covered with hundreds of various lights. Chandeliers large and small hung from golden chains. Countless lamps sat on thin tables along the wall, extending hundreds of feet before him until the corridor seemed to end in a blaze of light, as if leading directly into the sun. Everything was awash in a soothing yellow glow. Fred started forward, relishing the thick warm carpet beneath his bare feet. As he moved the air grew warmer. The sensation of warmth quickened his steps until he was all but jogging toward the open door in the distance. Then something strange began to happen. As he passed each lamp and chandelier he noticed that they went out. Not switched off, but snuffed out in an electric flash. He glanced over his shoulder and noticed that all the lights behind him had vanished, swallowed in a wave of darkness advancing at his heels. He spun around and ran faster, but the darkness was faster still, bulbs flashing out and smoking, some even exploding in a rain of sparks and glass one after another down the length of the corridor. He could not outrun them, though he ran now as fast as he could. A tidal wave of oily black swept past, ceiling, walls, and floor disappearing as if never there. Fred cried out and lunged for the last circle of light up ahead. Then, in a swirling rush, the final vestige of light, what just moments ago had been almost too bright to look at, was snuffed out as if it were no stronger than a candle. He screamed, lost his balance, and began to fall and fall and fall into nothing.

When he opened his eyes he knew at once it had been a nightmare. He breathed several deep breaths to calm himself before noticing something that was even worse than the dream.

His flashlight was still on, but the bulb was so dim now it gave off little more than a faint amber glow.

"No.....please no. Not now!" Fred banged it with the palm of his hand to no effect. He switched it off, then on. Off then on. But the light was in its final moments. Twenty seconds later, as he stared down helpless, the light grew fainter, and fainter, and fainter until it was no more. He squeezed the flashlight so tightly his skin ached.

And then the moaning resumed.

Fred lifted his head, gritted his teeth as fresh hot tears pushed out from his now-useless eyes. He was blind in the cave, and whatever moaned in the darkness was blocking his only route of escape.

# 16

Despair and utter hopelessness loomed over him, threatening to smother him.

Still clutching the flashlight, he tried desperately to ignore the moaning. With no light to guide him, he knew now there was little chance of his survival. He'd learned all too well that one misstep in the dark could mean a fall, broken bones, death. Any movement he made would be so slow as to be almost useless. He could try to go back, trace his path all the way to the cleft, where there was light and food. But it had nearly killed him before. Now, with no guiding illumination, it felt next to impossible. He was stuck in the depths of the earth, with a creature that would not stop making that dreadful noise.

His whole body felt ready to collapse. He slowly reached into his pocket and pulled out the last of the cricket pieces, now but a cluster of legs and crushed torsos. There was no taste to them, but at least he was eating, though the meal might be his last.

The moaning grew louder, rising to a quivering tone that sent chills over his entire body.

"What are you?" he shouted in the dark, his voice echoing off unseen walls. The moaning did not abate, did not even respond to his cry. He forced himself to stand up.

"You will not stop me," he said. "You will not keep me from moving on."

With a burst of courage that surprised him, Fred began to walk forward, not with small steps of caution, but with determined speed. Completely blind, he moved over the smooth stone floor and gave himself to whatever awaited. The moaning was so close now it blared in his ears.

Without warning, the floor dropped out from under him and he fell forward with arms flailing. He braced himself for the fatal crash, hoping to go quickly, but slammed onto slanted rock instead. It knocked the breath from his lungs and sent him rolling down an incline. When he finally slid to a stop seconds later, he groaned, awash with stabs of pain. When he tried to move, his right foot hit something loose. Not rock or stone. Something else. Something foreign.

The moaning was right before him now. He sat up and felt for the object with his hands. Immediately, he found something strange. It was smooth and slender, half an inch wide and a foot long. A tree limb? Searching further he found where it grew wide and bulbous, then split into two smaller branches. Following the object all the way down, the two smooth cylinders rejoined to another cluster of bumps then turned sharply at a right angle to several smaller branches, five in all, each ending at bony points.

His heart pounded as he realized what he was touching. Before he gave himself over to complete revulsion, he searched in the opposite direction and ran his hand upward until he found a pelvis, a spine, ribs, and then, to his horror, a skull with mouth gaping.

He lurched backward, kicking away from the corpse, but

the incline behind him did not allow him to go far. He had fallen into a kind of stony funnel, a mere five feet wide. He rolled onto his belly and tried frantically to claw his way up but it was no use. He slid back down within seconds. He was trapped.

Fred went motionless, tried to slow his breathing. A minute later he was able to calm down enough to think clearly. Right then, to his relief, the moaning stopped. All went quiet in the pit. When he garnered enough courage, he inched slowly forward to resume his examination.

A thin shred of fabric clung to some of the bones, rough and brittle. Almost like burlap. There were no shoes to be found. No jacket. No flashlight. He found a cluster of tightly wound twigs nearby and a satchel of some kind made of rawhide. It crumbled when he tried to open it. There was a sliver of stone inside with a sharpened edge, hewn to a point. Fred held the objects in his hands a moment as he realized what this was, who this was.

Was it a caveman? No. The bones would not have lasted so long in this condition. It must be a Native American. Centuries old. Had come down into the cave perhaps to explore, gotten lost, and died somehow.

Fred felt about for signs of injury and discovered a deep fracture on the back of its skull. The man had fallen just as he had fallen; but struck the back of his head on stone hard enough to kill him. He sat there beside the skeleton for some time without moving, imagined the day centuries ago when the man came down into the cave, holding up a torch of gathered twigs. How had he gotten down so deep? Had they come the same way? And how had he fallen? Had his torch gone out just as the flashlight had?

The boy raised his hand and placed it gently on the fleshless forehead.

"Why did you come down here?" he asked, expecting no answer.

For a long and somber while, Fred talked to the skull. He told it the story of his own adventure. And how he had managed to survive for so long. He found that as he talked, his heart became lighter in a way, as if the bones of that long-dead man, trapped like him, were listening sympathetically.

He spoke for a long time about Craig. What had happened back at camp, and about being pushed. His thoughts had not gone to the bully for days. Hadn't had time or space to. But now, as he pondered him, somehow, things were different. He no longer felt rage.

He felt pity.

What could drive someone to kill? What lies were twisted inside him? Fred didn't know. Couldn't know. But he did know what Craig had done up in the tunnel was the result of darkness in his own heart, a shadowed prison wrought from a thousand different wounds.

In a stab of memory he thought about what *he* had done. Digging up the underwear and bringing it into camp with no goal other than to humiliate. Fred closed his eyes, shook his head. The shame of such an act settled upon him like a cold ooze over his skin. It was a horrible thing to do. No matter what had happened before or after. And Fred had paid dearly, though the full price was still yet to be seen. If he'd managed to turn the other cheek, he would be home now, sleeping in his own warm, dry bed, talking with his parents, or reading his lovely arsenal of books. How strange that such a singular act can change everything, for good or ill. Granted, Craig's revenge was infinitely worse, but Fred was guilty as well. There seemed only one choice, one way forward, even if he never saw the light of day again.

He had no choice but to forgive. No choice but to let go. Even if he died in the cave and joined the bones with his own. He would not let his final days be poisoned with rage. He'd come too far for that.

A blast of air struck his face, followed by the loudest moan of all. He blinked in the dark as realization hit him. The moaning had not come from a creature at all, but from air currents whistling through the cave! Something about the stone funnel he was in caused the wind to moan as it passed through it. He grinned at his own ignorance, and then breathed in through his nose and smelled pine trees and honeysuckle. The air moving over him was warm!

"I'm close..." he said, voice rising. "I'm closer than ever."

Fred rose to his knees and leaned over the bones of the lost explorer. "I will find a way out...I will. And I will survive for the both of us."

He groped for the crumbling satchel, took the stone knife, and stepped over the bones to face whatever lay beyond.

# 17

The air pressed hard against him as he moved. He leaned into the current and took one careful step at a time. Aside from a series of gentle dips and rises, the tunnel remained steady and smooth. He held his good hand out in front of him like a mummy, sweeping it slowly from side to side to keep from running into some errant formation. When the air slowed and went still, he paused to listen for any new sounds. There was nothing of note. No sounds at least. But then, lingering in the stillness, he smelled something strange. Not the fresh outside smell borne on the wind, but something acrid. Like dirt, but more foul.

He started forward again, had just raised his hands as before, when he took a step into nothing, falling so suddenly there was no time to scream. One second, two seconds, three, rolling end over end in the dark. He squinted his eyes shut and hoped that death would come quickly. Air rushed up to meet him like a cushion and he felt he'd fallen forever when his body met the ground. A giant sledgehammer slammed up into his frame and his mind snapped out like an extinguished light.

When his eyes fluttered open some time later, he groaned at the fresh, acute pain in his arm. The fall had probably worsened the fracture. But how was he even alive? He'd fallen so far. When he felt beneath him his fingers dug into moistened dirt, or what felt like dirt. He raised his right hand to his nose and sniffed. Pungent, sulfuric, septic. His stomach turned in his belly. He swallowed. Fought back a gag. There was no mistaking what it was.

Bat guano.

Droppings, feces, dung.

And where such a pile existed, hundreds, thousands of bats were sure to exist as well, hanging from the ceiling above. He looked up pointlessly and listened. There was a faint, though constant cacophony of squeaks, a rustling of leathery wings, and a scraping of claws clinging to stone. Every second, something fell from above and landed on the pile where Fred sat wide-eyed with disgust, trapped in a rain shower of bat excrement.

He bent over in attempt to shield his head. A thousand thoughts of germs and disease and flesh-eating bacteria swirled within his mind. That single bat he had avoided now seemed like a joke, a trifle he would easily trade for what was happening to him now. Now there were countless hanging above him, and he was sinking into their latrine.

But their latrine had saved his life.

As soon as he mustered the strength, he pushed with his single functioning arm and slid down the guano pile on his bottom. It was a tall pile, several dozen feet at least from crest to base. When he reached hard, level stone he struggled to his feet and moved forward, much slower than before to keep from falling again. A second lifesaving pile of bat dung was highly unlikely. He would have to be more careful.

It wasn't long before his left arm began to swell. He could feel jagged bone cutting into muscle as he moved, though he tried hard to keep it stationary. If the injury was left untreated for much longer, things would not fare well for him, he knew.

The floor of the chamber angled down steadily, but not too steep for him to descend with ease. A new gust of air swept forward, this time colder and moist. He thought he could hear the distant roar of water rushing over stone. Was it a waterfall? An underground stream? Such a thing would likely lead to the outside world. The further he went the louder the sound became. His outstretched hand struck a wall and he turned to follow it as it angled to the left. The floor grew steeper. He clung to the wall as best he could but did not slow down. When a spray of water met his face, he knew he was very close.

Then something happened he had not prepared for. The stone beneath his feet had grown increasingly wet and slippery. More so than any he had walked upon since being in the cave. One moment he was walking as surefooted as a deer, and the next, his feet flew out from under him. He crashed on his back, banged the back of his head and began to slide, faster and faster and faster until there was no stopping. With a throat-rending cry, he rolled over and clawed at the moistened stone in attempt to stop himself.

"Please!" he screamed, but seemed only to accelerate. His nails split, his fingertips tore. "Please, God!"

And then, somehow, his fingers caught hold of a small knob and jolted him to a stop, right as his legs dangled off a ledge. Water roared deafening below, spray swirling up like inverted rain. He tried to pull himself up, but with only one arm it was no use. He tried to swing his legs onto the ledge but they were so weak, and the stone so wet, he could manage little more than few futile attempts.

His grip began to give way.

"Come on!" he shouted enraged, clenched his fingers upon the knob as tight as he could, but they continued to slip. Seconds more and he was done.

"All for this?" he shrieked, hot tears stark against the cold, drenching spray. "All for this?"

The face of his mother, his father, and the shining sun met his eyes in three sudden flashes.

And then he fell.

The plummet was not long, but the shocking cold when he struck the water was like a wall of spikes. He sank deep, spun round and round by eddies and currents impossible to fight. He'd failed to catch a breath before the river took him, and felt his lungs giving way within seconds. His head dimmed. His mouth gaped for air.

And then he was falling again, falling forever.

# 18

He awoke facedown on a shore of rounded stones, half his body still in the water. All was black, but he could hear the waterfall roaring behind him. He tried to roll over, but was stopped by a new injury. His left leg was limp and numb, like a piece of meat attached to his body. When he tried to move it searing bolts of pain drove him to cry out. Something was torn, or broken. He sunk his hands into the ground and squeezed them shut, sand and clay oozing between his fingers. With a broken arm he could still walk. But with an injured leg he would need a crutch. And searching for such a thing in the cave was futile, at best.

The tears that fell now were tinged with surrender. The cave had tried to kill him for so long in so many ways. But he had survived. He'd kept moving. Kept delving deeper. But now there was nothing left for him. For all his courage and risk, the darkness had beaten him. Fred's lip trembled bitterly.

"I'm sorry Mom...Dad," he whispered into the earth. "I tried."

For a long while he lay supine, trying to ignore the pain that wracked his entire body. His mind drifted to even darker places, imagining his bones joining that Indian's, to be found in a hundred years by a stranger. He reached down into his pocket and pulled out the stone knife. Just to hold it in his hand. He closed his eyes.

Through a haze of delirious slumber, the voice of his father drifted into his dreams. A memory he hadn't thought of in forever. Dad sitting on the edge of his bed one night years ago when Fred had cried in fear of the dark. With one hand, his father touched his head, and with the other he opened his leather-bound Bible and read.

*"Where can I go from your Spirit? Where can I flee from your presence? If I go up to the heavens, you are there; if I make my bed in the depths, you are there. If I rise on the wings of the dawn, if I settle on the far side of the sea, even there your hand will guide me, your right hand will hold me fast. If I say, 'Surely the darkness will hide me and the light become night around me,' even the darkness will not be dark to you; the night will shine like day, for darkness is as light to you."*

He opened his eyes, but knew he was still dreaming, for blue twilight was rising around him. He pressed his face down into the spongy earth. But the air grew brighter still, warmer, thick with summer smells. He lifted his head and saw that the dream had placed him in a forested gully, his body lying halfway in a pool with a waterfall at his back. Twenty feet away, a young doe nibbled on a patch of grass beside the water. It looked up and saw him, tilted its head, then dashed away with its white tail flagging. Soon the sun broke the horizon, blinding shafts slicing through a thousand shadows and bathing the forest in a yellow glow. Light reached the pool, reached his face and broken form, and he began to weep.

The dream was so real.

He expected it to vanish at any moment. Just as they all had. He expected to wake up and find himself blind and crippled in the belly of the earth, waiting to die. But the sun just kept rising.

*Was* this a dream?

He turned his head to look behind him and saw water gushing out of a ten-foot hole in the mountainside. It was the mouth of a cave. His cave.

It took a moment to sink in. But when it did, Fred began to laugh.

He'd ridden the river to freedom.

"Yes," he said, quiet at first, then growing into an all out shout. "Yes!"

He pulled himself out of the pool, dragging his leg beneath him. He took hold of a small oak tree growing near the water and pulled himself to his feet. Fire burned up and down his leg but he couldn't care less. He was out. He'd won.

"You see?" he shouted back at the cave, pounded his chest, reached down for a rock and threw it as hard as he could into the cavern's gaping mouth. The rock smashed onto stone somewhere inside. "You couldn't kill me!" he cried. "You lost!"

Fred stood there silent for quite some time as the waterfall roared before him, his mind going back to all the days he'd been trapped underground. The cold. The hunger. The dread. The danger. He'd beaten them all. He'd faced down a thousand Goliaths and won. He was different. Deep down he knew he wasn't the same boy he'd been before the cave, too scared to swim, too scared to climb. Too scared of everything.

"I won," he whispered once more.

He took the stone knife and went to work cutting an

inch-thick branch from a low-lying limb. He trimmed leaves and twigs away until he had a usable crutch. Shoving it under his good arm, he set out along the edge of the stream, picking his way between fallen logs and limestone boulders, feathered with lichen and moss. The going was not easy. But he felt more alive than he had his entire life.

After two hundred yards, the stream curved to the right, the gully leveled off and he found a clearly-marked hiking trail. This he took, moving as fast as his body would allow, and at times, even faster than was probably good for him. Five minutes later, the trail bisected a dirt road. He looked both ways, chose the right, and began hobbling, though his strength was finally giving way. He wouldn't be able to go much farther. And he had no idea how far it was to anything.

Right when he felt he had to rest, he heard the sound of an engine rumbling in the distance. Then tires crunching on gravel and country music blaring through open windows. The next moment, an old Chevy truck rounded a bend in the road ahead, plumes of red dust billowing up behind it. The driver slowed at the sight of him, then stopped. He was an old man, leathery as a saddle, hair white as cotton with a beard to his chest. He stuck his head out of the open window and frowned.

"You okay there, son?"

"I need a ride."

Minutes later, Fred sat in the truck as it rumbled up the road toward the highway. He leaned back against the headrest. It was the softest thing he'd felt in a long, long time.

The old man was talking fast through a thick country twang and a mouthful of tobacco. "I just about can't believe my eyes, son. Can't hardly believe you're sitting here beside me." He spat brown juice out the window, wiped his mouth with the back of a hand. "They searched for you for weeks. Had all kinds of cops and locals crawling all over the mountain. But it was like you up and vanished into thin air. Been all over the news. There was some kid from the city who they marked as suspect. But he swore up and down, crying like a baby he didn't know a thing. Said y'all were friends. That the last time he saw you was on a walk by Indian Creek...before you got separated. But they couldn't interrogate a kid for long without folks causing a stink." He looked over at Fred, who listened silently with eyes half closed and staring out the window. "So what really happened, kid? Where the heck have you been for the past two months?"

Fred could only breathe. In and out. Could only breathe and watch the light sifting through the trees like flashes of heaven. The old man furrowed his brow, turned his eyes back to the road.

"Are you thirsty?" the other asked. "I bet you're real thirsty after such an ordeal. Here..." He reached behind him where a small ice chest sat wedged against the seat. He opened the lid, groped about until he pulled out a small white carton dripping with ice-cold water.

"Hope you like milk."

Fred looked up at the carton, took it and held it in his hands. He swallowed dryly and opened one side, lifted it to his mouth. Before he drank he saw something printed on its side. A picture of a boy gone missing.

His eyes stared hard at the image.

He'd always hated that picture.

He shook his head, chuckled, and drank the carton dry.

## INTERVIEW WITH THE AUTHOR

***So why in the world did you write a story set in a cave?***

Great question! I've just always been strangely fascinated with them. My grandfather was a spelunker (that's just a fancy name for cave explorer) and I grew up searching out and exploring different caves in the Ozark mountains of Arkansas. Ever since I was a kid I've wondered what it would be like to be trapped in one for an extended period of time. I guess that makes me rather strange. But what writer isn't?

***How do you relate to Fred?***

Again, great question! Whoever wrote these is pretty astute. Anyways...about Fred. I *really* relate to him. In a way, you could say he's me. I used to deal with a lot of fear. To be honest, I still do sometimes. I also love books, though not quite as much as Fred does. His journey "through the dark" echoes a lot of my own journey learning to have courage and not listen to the voice of fear in my life.

***Why did you make Craig such an evil kid?***

I admit, he's a tad overdrawn. Then again, kids can be pretty darn brutal to each other. When I wrote Craig I couldn't help but think of his home life. What were his parents like? Were they abusive? I think it's safe to say all of Craig's volatility was merely the result of a great deal of pain elsewhere. With the boys on the camping trip, he felt powerful. He felt in control. When Fred took that away from him....well, it was like he lost everything. And we see what happened after that.

***What's the deal with the crow?***

Simple. The crow is the enemy. It comes in many forms. That evil force with the singular goal of destroying you. A lot of times our enemy can be inside our own heads speaking lies about ourselves and others and God. But I also believe in a real and dangerous unseen enemy spoken of in the Bible. He's called a thief...and all he wants to do is steal, kill, and destroy. I don't care to give him much attention other than to say God has already defeated him at the cross. All he can really do is lie to us. That's what the crow was trying to do to Fred....lie, lie, lie! But thankfully, our hero heard the voice of his Father (who, if you hadn't guessed, represents God Himself) and finally found light and freedom!

***What's the general "message" of this book?***

That's for you to ponder for yourself. Any good story should point you in the right direction and nudge you toward your own conclusions. Fred and Craig and the cave and the crow can mean a lot of different things to a lot of people. I say just give it some thought and let God teach you your own special lesson. Even as the author, I learned about fear and bitterness and the freeing power of forgiveness. Biggest of all, though, I learned about courage in the face of darkness. But don't take it from me.....

***Any more books on the way?***

You bet! I've already written a handful of new stories just waiting to get to print. Stay tuned! You won't be disappointed. There will be aliens, talking insects, and floating grill-cheese sandwiches. You know, standard stuff.

Made in the USA
Middletown, DE
12 January 2018